NO-ONE TO TURN TO

When she sees her husband Rob doing voluntary work with children, Chloe Marsden comes to a heart-breaking and life-changing decision. She forms a close bond with the Novak family after heavily pregnant Lauren is rushed off for emergency surgery. Things come to a head at Lexi Clarke's 21st birthday party at Laburnum Villa, when Chloe argues with Lauren. She's finally hit rock bottom, and feels that there is no one left to turn to. But she is wrong . . .

TERESA ASHBY

◆

NO-ONE TO TURN TO

Complete and Unabridged

LINFORD
Leicester

First published in Great Britain in 2023 by
D.C. Thomson & Co. Ltd.
Dundee

First Linford Edition
published 2023
by arrangement with the author and
D.C. Thomson & Co. Ltd.
Dundee

A catalogue record for this book is available
from the British Library.

ISBN 978–1–4448–5216–5

Published by
Ulverscroft Limited
Anstey, Leicestershire

Printed and bound in Great Britain by
TJ Books Ltd., Padstow, Cornwall

This book is printed on acid-free paper

Morning Run

Lexi never tired of watching the sun rise over the sea. Every morning was different, but in winter it was at its most stunning.

Today the sun was peeping out from behind clouds it had lined with what looked like purest gold. It was a sight that never failed to lift Lexi's spirits.

She stopped running for a moment and breathed in the bracing sea air. Busy oyster-catchers scurried along amongst the gulls and, with the tide out, hundreds of geese lined up along the edge of the water.

Behind her the Beach Hut, shop and home to the caretakers of the beach houses, was in darkness.

Three years ago, when she and her sister Beth had arrived here and Beth had taken over the running of the Beach Hut, Lexi had been a stroppy eighteen-year-old.

Furze Point was the last place she'd

wanted to be.

So much had changed. Beth had married Noah Walsh and they'd transformed the once-derelict Laburnum Villa into a centre for chiropractic and other therapies.

Lexi had left university to move in with Rachel Taylor and help her to run the Tiny Tails rescue centre. Somewhere along the line Lexi had fallen in love with Furze Point.

Eighteen-year-old Lexi wouldn't have dreamed of going for a run in the mornings but life had real purpose now. She felt part of the community here, of a big family.

She even had a set of honorary grandparents in Tom and Carol Bennett who lived in Corky's Cottage in the grounds of Laburnum Villa.

Everything was right with her world. She was enjoying life and was filled with hope for the future.

She started to run again. Today she would go all the way to Laburnum Villa, which could be accessed from the beach further along, so she could check in on Beth.

Her smile was momentarily replaced by a worried frown. She hadn't seen much of her sister lately and when she did, Beth had seemed distracted.

Lexi hoped there was nothing wrong between her and Noah.

She stopped to be greeted by Gemma, a beautiful Labrador belonging to Rob and Chloe Marsden. Chloe was wrapped up in a white padded jacket and black leggings.

She had her hood up and the fake-fur trim framed her elfin face.

'Gemma! Come back here! Lexi doesn't want to be covered in sand.'

'Too late!' Lexi laughed. 'I don't mind.'

'Some would,' Chloe said. 'One day Gemma went for a swim then shook herself near a family from one of the beach houses. Honestly, you'd have thought she'd pebble-dashed them the way they carried on.

'They accused me of having an out-of-control dog.'

'Gemma? Out of control? She wouldn't harm anyone. Are you OK, Chloe? You're up very early and you look tired.'

Chloe's eyes were red and had bags under them. Always petite, right now she looked tiny and worn down.

'Thanks,' she muttered snippily.

'I'm sorry, that sounded awful! You always look so pretty. I was just worried about you, that's all.'

'I didn't sleep very well,' Chloe admitted, her face softening as she reached out and squeezed Lexi's arm. 'I'm just a bit . . .'

She broke off and stared out over the sea.

'I don't know. I can't remember the last time I had a decent night's sleep.'

'How's it going at the gallery? Dominic said you've made space for more of his paintings.'

Chloe's face lit up.

'Yes! Word is getting round about his talent. I can't wait to see what he's got for me. On that note, I'd best crack on. Lovely to see you, Lexi.'

4

'You, too.'

Chloe clicked her fingers and the Labrador fell into step beside her.

Lexi watched them walk away. She bit her lip. Something was wrong with Chloe. She wasn't striding as confidently as usual and there was a stoop to her shoulders.

Chloe and Rob always seemed happy and the gallery was doing well. She just hoped Chloe wasn't ill.

She started to run again. Picking up the pace she jogged past the beach houses which stood up on stilts and had been built into the low cliff.

They were all empty. The owners tended to use them mainly in summer.

She found the pathway that cut up from the beach and, with one last burst of energy, ran up the steep slope.

Since the house had been renovated the pathway had been made more accessible. She didn't have to fight her way through the undergrowth to get to the gardens as she had the first few times she'd used it.

Beth's new assistant, Marie, was turning out the horses into the paddocks. She gave Lexi a wave.

It used to be either Lexi or Fergus that saw to the horses and Lexi had felt a bit sidelined at first, but at least she had more time for rescue work and dog grooming.

She was also training to be a pet hydrotherapist.

'What's that look for?' Beth had asked when she told Lexi she'd taken Marie on. 'I could have offered the job to you but you wouldn't have wanted it.'

'How do you know?'

'Because I know you!'

Beth had laughed and, eventually, Lexi had got off her high horse and joined in. Her sister was right. Lexi was busy charting her own course in life.

Sisters

Beth was sitting at the huge kitchen table with her laptop open and papers spread out all over the place. She was still in her dressing-gown.

'You look busy,' Lexi commented.

Beth jumped, then slammed the laptop shut and gathered up all the papers hastily into a folder.

'What are you doing here so early?' she snapped.

Lexi felt stung. Normally Beth was pleased to see her.

'Sorry. I'll go, shall I?'

There was a rush of tears to her eyes at Beth's reaction. She felt very hurt and wouldn't mind betting Beth didn't speak to Marie like that.

The wonderful feeling of wellbeing and belonging she'd felt a few minutes before evaporated like sea mist in the sunshine.

'No, don't go!' Beth stood up and hurried after her. 'Sorry, Lexi. I was miles away, engrossed in something. Time just got away from me.

'I should be showered and dressed by now but I wanted to . . . never mind.'

Lexi refused for a moment to return Beth's hug, then told herself she was imagining things and wrapped her arms round her sister.

'You're OK?' Beth asked.

'Absolutely,' Lexi replied.

'You look all rosy cheeked and healthy,' Beth observed. 'The daily run is doing you good.'

Lexi cast a look at the laptop and the folder as they stopped hugging. Beth had been in a hurry to hide it all.

What was it?

'Is something wrong?'

'No, it's nothing to worry about.' Beth smiled. 'Just a function I'm arranging.'

'Another wedding?'

'No. Anyway, how are you?'

Wow, that was a fast change of subject! A brush off?

Again Lexi felt a sense of unease, as if she wasn't really welcome here.

8

Normally Beth was only too pleased to share things with her and she had often asked her opinion.

Why the sudden secrecy?

Her eyes strayed to the folder. Some of the papers were poking out as well as the tip of a photograph.

'Coffee?' Beth offered.

'You know me!' Lexi grinned.

'I could do with a break. Take a seat.'

Beth had no sooner turned her back than Lexi sat down at the table and poked at the image with her finger, drawing it out.

The person in the photograph looked like her . . . It was her! An old school photo from years ago, before their mother had died.

Lexi looked at that young face, all cheery and freckly, and felt a pang of sorrow. The girl in the photograph had no idea about what was coming — which was probably just as well.

She didn't remember her dad, who had died when she was two. Their mum had worked all hours and had seemed indestructible.

Sadly she wasn't and was killed crossing the road when Lexi was eight, not long after that photo was taken.

'Have you had breakfast?'

Lexi poked the photo back quickly. What was her sister up to?

She knew that Beth and Noah were interested in family history. Had Beth found something she didn't want Lexi to know about?

'Lexi, are you hungry?'

'Starving!'

'Porridge?'

No-one made porridge like Beth — except their mum, of course. Lexi felt another pang of sorrow for what she'd lost.

'What's wrong?'

'I was just thinking about the porridge Mum used to make.'

'Aw, love.' Beth gave her another hug. 'I think Mum would be proud of us, don't you?'

'Proud of you, maybe,' the young girl replied. 'You're the one with the huge house and rich husband!'

'Ouch!' Beth cried. 'Noah's not rich.'

'Come off it! He gets left this mansion by his grandmother and has enough put by to do it up and turn it into a chiropractic and therapy clinic.'

'We had to borrow money, Lexi, and we both work hard.'

'Sorry, I shouldn't have said that. I didn't mean it.'

'Don't worry. Anyway, Mum always said that the thing that made her proudest of us at school was when our report cards mentioned that we were kind to others.

'Now look at you, rescuing animals! I think Mum would be delighted.'

'I can't remember what she looked like,' Lexi confessed. 'I have to try really hard to picture her face.

'Unless I look at a photo I just can't see her in my mind. All I see is a sort of outline with blurred features.

'Yet I remember the taste of her porridge. It's crazy.'

'It's not crazy. I'm the same. It's not

that you're forgetting her.'

'What did Dad die of, Beth?'

'I don't know; I was only twelve. All I know is that I came home from school and a neighbour was looking after you.

'Mum was up in her bedroom and I'd never seen her so upset before. She told me Dad had died suddenly but she never said any more than that.

'When Mum died I tried to find out where Dad was buried so they could be laid to rest together but I couldn't.'

'You were only eighteen,' Lexi marvelled. 'I don't know how you coped.'

'I did what I had to do,' Beth replied. 'So, porridge?'

Lexi couldn't help thinking that Beth was as bad as their mother had been when it came to not talking about things.

She wasn't going to push it, though. What would be the point?

Nevertheless she couldn't get rid of the feeling that her sister was keeping something from her.

Back Home

Later that day Anna held tight to Fergus as he turned the Harley-Davidson into the car park outside the Bluebell Farm Shop.

Nisha, Fergus's capable assistant, was in the process of closing up for the night. She began to jump up and down when she saw them coming.

'You're back!' she shouted as Anna dismounted and took off her crash helmet, fluffing up her blonde hair with her fingers. 'How was the holiday? Did you have a wonderful time?'

Before Anna could speak, Fergus drove the Harley into the barn then bustled off to check on his beloved animals.

'Is he OK?' Nisha asked.

'He was worrying about Myfanwy,' Anna said. 'I know he called a couple of times while we were away to check on her.'

'A couple of times?' Nisha laughed. 'Try half a dozen! He's never spent so much as a night away from the farm before, to be fair. I'm amazed he trusted me to look after things here.'

'He does trust you, Nisha,' Anna assured her. 'I know he kept checking up but he wouldn't have left this place in the hands of anyone else.'

Nisha crossed her arms and smiled.

'You've a smile on your face the size of a small village,' she pointed out. 'I can tell you I wouldn't be smiling after sitting on the back of a motorbike all the way home from the Lake District.'

'It wasn't too bad,' Anna said. 'A bit unpleasant when it rained, mind you.'

'He'll be checking on the feral cats now,' Nisha said. 'If he's finished cuddling Myfanwy!'

They both laughed again. Fergus's love for his animals was legendary and especially for Myfanwy, the cow, who was from his late father's dairy herd.

Fergus had turned the dairy farm into an organic farm after his father's death. As well as having his own beasts living out their retirement years he'd added to them with a number of rescues.

'How has it been here? I know we've only been away a few days but it feels like a lifetime. Anything exciting happen?'

'Not really,' Nisha said. 'Though Dylan and I have decided to rent a flat together.'

'That's wonderful!'

Dylan was a nurse at the practice where Anna worked as a vet and he and Nisha had been friends for years.

'It's nothing like that,' Nisha said quickly. 'We're just good friends. We've taken the flat over the antiques shop.'

'I thought the shop had been sold,' Anna said. 'It was empty last time I went past.'

'A new woman owns it, Angela Chapman. She's quite a character.

'She bought the house next door to the shop and is living there with her son, Oliver. She didn't want the hassle of a holiday let so agreed to let the flat to us.'

'Wow, it's all been happening!'

Anna's heart leaped as she saw Fergus making his way back. A couple of his rescue hens trotted at his heels like feathery dogs. Clearly they were as happy to see him as he was to see them.

She felt so lucky to have him in her life. Her gentle giant.

'Have you told her the news?' Fergus asked as he reached them.

'What news?' Nisha asked.

'I thought you'd like to do the honours.'

Anna had to suppress a wave of excitement rising inside her. If Fergus didn't say something soon she'd burst with it.

'Tell me what?' Nisha demanded. 'Come on, what have you been up to? You haven't got lots more animals coming, have you?

'Oh, no! You're going to sell Bluebell Farm!'

Anna laughed.

'Have you actually met my husband?'

Nisha looked puzzled.

'I didn't know you were married.'

Fergus reached for Anna's hand.

'Anna is married,' he said. 'To me! Meet the new Mrs Thompson!'

'You're married?' Nisha cried. 'You're married! How? When? Where?'

'The usual way,' Fergus said calmly. 'Three days ago. Gretna Green.'

'You said you were going to the Lake District.'

'We did,' Anna agreed. 'Fergus came to meet my parents, then Dad drove us to Gretna Green.'

'That's so romantic!' Nisha said. 'But how could you?'

'Sorry?'

'If we'd known we would have had a huge celebration for you.

'Still, it's not too late. I'll have a word with Beth and see what we can organise.

'Perhaps we could have the reception in the grounds of Laburnum Villa when the weather is better.'

'Whoa! Hold your horses,' Fergus protested, looking terrified. 'No party. The reason we went away to tie the knot was because we didn't want any fuss.'

'It's not our thing, Nisha,' Anna explained. 'It was perfect with just us and my parents.'

Nisha shook her head then hugged them both.

'I understand,' she said even though, probably, she didn't.

If she were to get married no doubt she'd want to shout it from the rooftops!

'Congratulations anyway. I'm so happy for you.'

'Please don't tell anyone else for now,' Anna said. 'I haven't told my brother yet.

'I'm going to pop round tomorrow to tell him that I'll be moving out of the cottage and it'll be all theirs if they want it.'

'You didn't even tell Nick?' Nisha gasped.

Anna shook her head.

She hadn't been too sure about what to do. She knew, if she told them, he and Lauren would have wanted to plan something. Lauren had enough on her plate with the pregnancy.

Besides, then she would have had to tell her sister who would have wanted to come to the wedding.

'He'll be all right with it.' Anna bit her

18

lip. 'Yes, I'm sure he will. They're very happy and settled in the cottage.

'The only difference will be that I won't be there and they'll have the place to themselves!'

'You can get off home, if you like, Nisha,' Fergus suggested. 'You've been working hard while we've been away.'

'I didn't mind a bit,' she assured him. 'It was fun being in charge. But I will go home now and leave you two lovebirds on your own.

'I stocked up the fridge with a few bits and pieces for you so you won't have to worry about going shopping or anything like that.

'You can just enjoy the next few days together.'

'That was very thoughtful of you,' Anna said. 'Thank you, Nisha.'

She had intended to visit her brother as soon as they got back. She couldn't wait to see him, Lauren and Casey and all her dogs.

Right now, however, she was overcome with a feeling of contented weariness, if such a thing existed.

Yes, very tired, but in a wonderful, settled sort of way. It felt right to spend the first evening and night in their home as a married couple quietly and without any fuss.

'You're Not Well'

The following afternoon Chloe Marsden was working in the gallery when she saw heavily pregnant Lauren Novak walk past.

She stopped for a moment and rested her head against the glass. Chloe assumed she was admiring Dominic's paintings but it became clear that something was wrong.

Tears were running down Lauren's face, which was near grey.

She rushed out and Lauren jumped back, startled.

'Sorry! I think I have left handprints on your window and your windows are always so . . .' Her face twisted and she cried out.

'Come inside,' Chloe said, taking Lauren's arm. 'Sit down for a minute. Is there anyone I can call for you? Is Anna back from her trip yet?'

'She's due back today,' Lauren replied, 'and Nick's at work but I'm fine, I really am. It's nothing, just Braxton Hicks.'

'False labour pains?' Chloe asked.

'Yes, though real enough!' Lauren said with a wry smile. 'It's just the body practising, I think. You know how it is.'

Chloe wished with all her heart that she did know. She and Rob had been trying for years for a baby. They'd been through every kind of fertility treatment and several failed attempts at IVF.

It had all got too much for Rob. He'd sat her down and said enough was enough.

It was what it was and they should concentrate on enjoying their lives and not spend every spare moment thinking about babies.

They had each other and were happy and they should just be content with that.

Then he'd turned round and said perhaps they should consider adoption! So clearly he hadn't given up.

Adoption wasn't easy and Chloe wasn't sure she could take any more disappointments. Besides, how could she love a child that wasn't her own?

Wouldn't it be a constant reminder of what she couldn't have?

Rob had been right, of course, about calling time on their efforts to become pregnant. It had driven Chloe almost to breaking point.

She'd become obsessed with watching her weight as well as Rob's, thinking that might have some kind of bearing on things.

Even Gemma, her dog, had been put on a strict diet.

It was as if Chloe was trying to control everything simply because she had no control over her own body.

She looked down at Lauren who was sitting on the chair, breathing deeply. She had a little more colour in her cheeks.

Gemma was at her side, her head resting on Lauren's knee, concern in her gentle eyes.

'Are you sure you're all right, Lauren? You were crying.'

'Yes, I'll be fine,' Lauren said although she looked far from fine. 'Blame my hormones! I'm all over the place.

'I'm just on my way down to the front to fetch Casey. She's been doing a beach litter-pick with some other children from school.'

Chloe looked into the gallery and bit her lip. She couldn't leave Lauren to walk down there on her own.

'Rob's down there helping out with that,' she said. 'I'll walk with you, if that's OK. I'll just get Gemma's lead.'

'You don't have to do that!' Lauren protested. 'I'll be fine.'

'I was planning to take her for a walk,' Chloe soothed.

Gemma came alive when she saw her lead, never mind that she'd had a good run not long ago.

Chloe's heart was pounding. She was worried about Lauren. What was wrong seemed to be more than she was letting on. There was no way Chloe was leaving her to walk to the beach alone.

Lauren made a fuss of Gemma while Chloe locked up, then they walked together down to the seafront.

They could see groups of children in hi-vis jackets laughing as they brought their full bin bags to the skip.

'It's amazing, isn't it?' Lauren remarked. 'Ask a child to pick up something they've dropped and you get grumbles.

'Send them to pick up other people's rubbish and they can't wait!'

'Oh, I can't believe Casey is like that,' Chloe argued.

'No, not really,' Lauren said. 'But she will occasionally scrunch up a crisp packet and just leave it on the arm of the sofa or drop something and not bother picking it up.'

Chloe spotted five-year-old Casey whose bright red curls stood out. When she saw them coming she waved furiously.

Lauren waved back then stumbled.

Chloe grabbed her arm.

'You're not all right, are you?'

'I don't feel too well,' Lauren admitted. 'It's probably a bug. I'll be fine.'

'I wish you'd let me call Nick.'

'Absolutely not. He'll only fuss.'

Casey was in Rob's group. He was there in his capacity as an RNLI volunteer and the kids with him all looked happy.

Also helping out were Jamie and Rosita Tennyson from the Lighthouse Café and Lexi's sister, Beth, from Laburnum Villa.

Rob turned, saw Chloe and waved, his face lighting up. When she thought of how she'd nagged him about his eating habits her stomach clenched. She was so lucky to have him.

One of the children was tugging on his sleeve and he squatted down to talk to him.

'Your Rob is so good with kids, isn't he?' Lauren said. 'Casey has been attending his swimming lessons. It's a shame he . . .'

'Go on, say it,' Chloe snapped. 'I know it's what you're thinking. It's what everyone thinks, including me!'

'I was going to say it's a shame he's not a teacher,' Lauren said, looking

26

confused. 'I bet he'd make a brilliant one. What did you think I was going to say, Chloe?'

'Nothing.' She shrugged. 'Sorry.'

Rob came across to them holding Casey's hand. Gemma rushed to greet him and he seemed as pleased to see her as she was to see him.

'Casey has been very helpful,' he told Lauren. 'She must have picked up her weight in rubbish today. If you're not in a hurry the local paper wants everyone to pose for a photo.'

'That's fine,' Lauren said. 'We have plenty of time.'

When he'd gone Chloe led Lauren to a bench.

'You should sit down. You don't look at all well.'

'You can talk!' Lauren replied. 'Have you seen yourself? You look so tired, Chloe.'

'You're not the first person to say that,' Chloe admitted, remembering Lexi's concern. 'I've just not been sleeping well. I have a lot on my mind.'

Chloe turned her gaze to Rob, once again surrounded by kids as he tried to get them together for a photo. He looked so happy with them jumping round him like excited puppies.

She squeezed her eyes shut.

Adoption could take years. Wouldn't it be better to walk away now so he could make a fresh start with someone who could give him the family he deserved?

The laughter and shouts of the kids startled her.

'Whoever would have thought litter-picking could be so much fun?' Lauren said.

'Anything can be fun with the right person,' Chloe murmured. 'Lauren, would you like Rob to drive you home from here? It'll save you a walk up the hill.'

Lauren's eyes filled with tears and she bit her lip.

'That would be amazing,' she whispered. 'The thought of walking home was really getting me down.

'How stupid! Normally I'd walk anywhere without even thinking about it.'

'Rob has a couple of booster seats in the car,' Chloe told her, 'so Casey can sit safely. He's always ferrying other people's kids about.'

She hadn't meant those words to come out as criticism but Lauren didn't seem to notice.

The photoshoot was over and now the kids were still bouncing round Rob like rubber balls, all trying to get his attention as he handed out lollipops.

'He's far and away the most popular guy around here,' Lauren decided. 'Casey adores him.'

'Everyone loves Rob,' Chloe said.

She could only dream about how much his own children would adore him.

But that was all it would be as long as they stayed married. Just a dream.

Drifting Apart

The children were handed back to their parents and Rob brought Casey back. The stick of a lollipop poked out of his mouth. Casey was gripping hers tightly.

'You shouldn't walk with a lolly in your mouth,' Chloe scolded. 'What if you fell? You're not setting a good example.'

Rob looked chastened and pulled the stick out. Chloe saw Casey flash him a look of sympathy.

'Chloe's right,' Lauren chipped in. 'It can be very dangerous.'

'I didn't walk with a lolly in my mouth, Mummy,' Casey pointed out.

'I know,' Rob said. 'Chloe's right, as always. I'm sorry.'

Chloe felt a rush of sympathy for him. He'd taken unpaid time off work to do the litter pick and now she'd made him feel bad.

'Make sure you brush your teeth to get rid of all the sugar when you've finished, Rob. You don't want any more fillings.'

Rob and Casey exchanged looks and burst out laughing.

'You may think it's funny but you'll thank me when all your teeth don't fall out.'

'Come on, Casey, we should get going,' Lauren said.

'Wait. Rob, I said we'd give Lauren and Casey a lift home.'

'Sure. Are you coming, too?'

Chloe nodded. She wanted to hug Rob and tell him how much she loved him, but it felt as if they were drifting steadily away from each other.

They didn't talk like they used to and when she did talk to him it was to criticise.

Perhaps her subconscious was already pushing him away, making him want to leave so she didn't have to tell him to go.

Gemma hopped into the back of the car and Chloe sat in the back with Casey.

Rob held the door for Lauren to get in the front. He put his hand out to steady her.

'Are you OK?'

Chloe was about to snap that Lauren was pregnant, not ill, but bit it back.

'A bit tired,' Lauren conceded.

It was more than that, though. Her wincing and little groans of pain hadn't gone unnoticed by Chloe.

When they reached Anna's cottage Chloe went inside with Lauren and Casey while Rob turned the car round.

'Thank you for this,' Lauren said.

'No problem.' Chloe leaned closer. 'Would you like me to call Nick?'

'What for?'

'I'm worried about you.'

'I'll be fine,' Lauren assured her. 'Nick has enough to worry about.'

Chloe nodded. She'd heard that Nick had transferred to maternity and that they were very short-staffed.

'Promise you'll call me if you need anything,' Chloe said. 'You have my number?'

'I think I have everyone's number. This place!' She laughed. 'I feel as if I've been adopted!'

'You have,' Chloe replied. 'That's how

it works around here.'

'You've been especially nice to me, Chloe. Thank you. I appreciate it.'

As Chloe went back to the car her heart gave a surge when she saw Rob waiting for her, smiling as if she hadn't been snapping his head off.

The town would look after him when they split up. His friends would help.

He opened the window and waved something.

'Casey left her hat behind. It was in my pocket. Trying to get the kids to keep their hats on was a nightmare!'

Chloe ran back up the path with it just as Casey was coming out to ask if Rob had it. She took the hat and hugged Chloe.

Even after the little girl had gone in and closed the door Chloe couldn't move. When she did turn back to the car, Rob was watching her, frowning.

His best friends were Noah from up at Laburnum Villa and dear Fergus at Bluebell Farm. They'd rally round and give him the support he needed.

Chloe wouldn't need support. She had to be as cold blooded as possible about this.

Rob's face broke into a smile which began to waver as she got into the car. 'Everything OK?'

He looked so worried that she longed to reassure him but mustn't.

'I don't think so, Rob. Things haven't been right between us for quite a while.'

'I meant with Lauren.'

'Not sure but I've told her to call me if she needs anything. I can't do more than that.

'I should have realised you weren't talking about us.'

He started the car and looked at the road ahead, his jaw set. He'd gone silent on her again.

That was what he did lately. She snapped, he went quiet and the distance between them widened a little more.

A Dark Time

Lauren was peeling the vegetables for dinner when the front door opened.

'Anna?' she called out. 'Is that you?'

She wasn't sure if Anna would be back in time for dinner although she'd heard that she and Fergus had got back yesterday.

It seemed odd. Why hadn't Anna come home?

'It's me.' Nick appeared.

'What are you doing home? Has something happened?'

'Yes, something has happened,' he said, pulling her into his arms.

'What is it?'

He kissed the top of her head.

'It's you,' he said at last. 'Chloe called me. She's worried about you, Lauren.'

She sighed with irritation.

'Have you actually met Chloe?' Lauren said. 'She's lovely but you have to admit she's a bit controlling. Go back to the hospital where you're really needed.'

'It's quiet at the moment,' he replied as he led her through to the sitting-room. 'They'll call if they need me and I can be there in a few minutes.

'I want you to sit down and put your feet up while I sort out dinner. Where's Casey? How did her litter-pick go?'

'She's in her room. Well, it's not really her room, is it? Oh, I'm sorry that I sound ungrateful and grumpy.

'I was hoping we'd be settled in our own place before the baby came.'

She bit her lip as pain pulsated through her abdomen.

'What was that?'

Nick was so perceptive. There was no hiding anything from him.

'I'm fine,' she lied.

'You're not. You don't look fine at all. You're very pale, Lauren.

'What are you not telling me? It's more than us not having our own place yet.'

'Take no notice of me.' She tried to wave away his concern. 'I'm just feeling grouchy and fed up. You know how it is. Pregnancy hormones and all that.'

Nick pushed a footstool over and lifted Lauren's feet on to it with such tender care that it brought a lump to her throat.

'That's better,' he suggested.

'I'm glad you think so but I've got things to do, Nick, and you've just come off a double shift!'

'Which I didn't finish,' he argued.

'Don't split hairs. You're the one who should be putting your feet up, not me! You can't wrap me in bubble wrap.'

'Try to stop me!' He laughed.

She sighed and tried to look cross but couldn't stop a smile. Nick had initially trained as a midwife but his last job had been for an agency as he tried to make enough money so that Lauren didn't have to work once the baby was born.

Then he'd hit on the idea of moving to Furze Point — not just to be close to his sister but also because housing was cheaper.

Not long after he started work at the hospital an opening had come up in the little maternity unit and he was back doing the job he really loved.

Being the only midwife at the unit, however, he got called in at all sorts of hours.

The pace of life was slower here and Lauren had been able to leave her stressful job. She'd have to find a part-time job once the baby came but right now she could rest as much as she needed.

Life was good — and she was fine!

'I'm not an invalid, Nick,' she insisted.

'Daddy!' A shout went up and Casey, came hurtling down the stairs. 'You're home!'

He swept her up in his arms and twirled her around. The joy on his face brought a lump to Lauren's throat. Nick was such a lovely dad.

All he wanted was to look after them and if she let him have his way she'd never have to lift a finger.

'How was school?' he asked.

'Great! I did you a picture.'

She wriggled to get down and ran off to find the painting.

'Stop treating me as if I'm fragile, Nick,' Lauren said, pushing the footstool away and struggling to her feet. 'This isn't going to be like it was with Casey and, even if it was, putting my feet up wouldn't stop that happening.'

His shoulders sagged.

'I know. I just want to look after you.'

Lauren had had post-natal depression after Casey was born and part of her worried it would happen again. It had been a very dark time in her life.

Just when she should have been enjoying her new baby she'd become convinced that she wasn't good enough and that Casey would be taken away.

She shivered, remembering how vulnerable and insecure she'd felt.

It wasn't going to be like that this time.

'I feel as fit as a flea. Full of energy and raring to go.'

His eyebrows shot up.

'Are you really?'

'A couple of twinges don't mean anything,' she said. 'I'm not due for another two weeks and I don't feel I'm about to go into labour.'

She went back with him into the kitchen.

Casey joined them with her picture. She had an amazing talent when it came to drawing and painting.

'This is great, Casey!' Nick said. 'We'll put it on the wall. It's our family, isn't it?'

'Yes, this is you and that's Mummy. That one is me and I'm holding the new baby.'

'Perfect.' He put the picture up on the kitchen wall with all the others.

'Do you think Anna minds us sticking pictures all over her walls?' Lauren asked.

'She suggested it. My sister is very impressed with her artistic niece. As are we! I don't know where she gets it from.'

'We mustn't forget that this is Anna's home and we are just guests in it.'

'She said it was our home for as long as we needed,' he reminded her. 'As we haven't found anywhere suitable yet it is what it is. If the walls are damaged I'll repaint them when we leave.'

'I wonder when she'll be home,' Lauren mused, checking her watch. 'I can't wait to hear about their holiday.'

'It was all very mysterious and last-minute, wasn't it? I think perhaps things must be very serious between them if Anna took them to meet Mum and Dad.

'Fergus seems quite old fashioned. Do you think he asked for her hand in marriage?'

Lauren laughed.

'Stop over-thinking things, Nick,' she said. 'Come on. We can make dinner together.'

She thought perhaps it was best not to mention the odd, niggling pain in her side that was radiating across her stomach. Nick would only worry.

You'd think, him being a professional,that no pregnancy would faze him at all, but he was different with her.

It was fine. She'd done a lot of cleaning and had probably just pulled a muscle, or the baby was pressing on a nerve.

She really didn't want to make any fuss about it.

Casey took over the conversation, telling Nick all about the litter she'd picked up and how Rob had made her laugh.

It was good to have his attention taken away from Lauren.

'Something's Wrong'

It was early evening when Anna pulled up outside the cottage and saw Nick's car parked outside. She'd made him promise to let her know if Lauren had the baby while she was away but had heard nothing.

She was looking forward to married life at the farm and Nick and Lauren would be pleased to have the cottage to themselves, especially when the baby arrived.

At least now they could take their time looking for somewhere else if they wanted to. If they preferred to stay put they could get their own furniture out of storage and make the place their own.

'Auntie Nan!'

Casey squealed as Anna walked in and ran into her arms.

Anna held her tight. She would miss her little niece but she'd still see plenty of her.

There was a stampede of dogs down

the hall and Anna greeted them all, wondering if they had missed her as much as she'd missed them.

They'd love living at the farm! They'd be around people all day if they wanted to be and they knew how to behave around the other animals.

'We've just eaten!' Nick called from the kitchen. 'I can rustle something up for you, if you like.'

'Nothing for me, thanks.'

Nick emerged from the kitchen wiping his hands on a towel.

'Coffee, then?'

'Lovely.'

'Lauren's in the sitting-room. I'll be through in a minute.'

She went through and saw her sister-in-law sitting with her feet up. She looked pale.

'Are you OK, Lauren?'

'I've been busy,' Lauren said with a smile that was apologetic. 'I didn't want you coming home to a mucky house.

'Nick thinks I've been nest-building and that the baby's arrival is imminent. I didn't eat much at dinner, either, which has convinced him even more.'

'You shouldn't have tired yourself out cleaning!' Anna protested. 'Not on my account.'

'Never mind all that. Did you have a lovely time?'

Anna sat down next to her sister-in-law and held her hand. Lauren squeezed and gasped softly.

'Is this it?' Anna asked.

'I don't know. It doesn't feel like it did with Casey,' Lauren whispered. 'The pain is different and I don't feel well.

'Something's not right. Or am I worrying over nothing?'

'Have you told Nick?'

'Told Nick what?' He came in with the coffee and a glass of juice for Lauren.

'Tell him,' Anna ordered. 'If you don't I will.'

'I've got a pain and I feel a bit sick,' Lauren admitted.

'What sort of pain? Where? Why didn't you say?'

'I didn't want to because I knew you'd

panic!' Lauren said, wincing. 'I know you're a nurse but you go into helpless-husband mode if you think anything is wrong.'

Nick certainly looked as if the cool-headed, professional persona had abandoned him for a moment, but he took a deep breath.

'Plus I wanted to wait until I knew Anna was back,' Lauren added.

Anna was filled with guilt. She should have come home last night instead of basking in married life.

Nick turned to Anna.

'Would you fetch Lauren's bag, please? It's in our bedroom. Casey will show you where it is.

'She helped Mummy pack, Auntie Nan, isn't that great? I'm going to call the unit and I'm taking you in, Lauren.'

'I think it's just a bit of indigestion or a pulled muscle,' Lauren argued. 'I don't want to go to hospital yet, Nick.'

'The worst that can happen is that it's a false alarm and they'll send us home,' he soothed.

46

'I'll feel like an idiot.'

'No, you won't. False alarms happen all the time. We'd rather someone came in unnecessarily than they ended up giving birth in a car on the way or on the kitchen floor!'

'At least if that happened I'd have my own personal midwife to look after me!'

Anna hurried upstairs with Casey, her heart pounding. Something felt wrong. Lauren was trying to stay casual but it didn't quite gel.

'Mummy is going to have the baby and come straight home,' Casey told her. 'We packed snacks and drinks and things for the baby to wear to come home. I chose them.

'Will you stay with me until they get back? Do you think they'll be back by bedtime?'

'Sometimes it takes a while to have a baby,' Anna replied. 'But if they come home and you're asleep I promise I'll wake you. Of course I'll stay with you! I would never leave you on your own, Casey.'

By the time they got downstairs Nick was leading Lauren down the hall. He cast an anxious look at Anna then smiled at Casey.

'Isn't it exciting?' he told her. 'When we come home we may have your baby brother or sister. Then Nanny and Grandad will come to stay for a while.'

'Good luck.' Anna hugged Lauren.

Nick didn't know it yet but there would be a spare bedroom for their parents to use when they came down.

'Not that you'll need it. Everything is going to be just fine,' she added.

'Will you . . . ?' Nick began.

'I'll take care of Casey till you get home,' Anna agreed. 'I've a few more days off left. Call me as soon as there's news.'

Lauren looked small and scared as Nick helped her into the car.

Anna reached in and squeezed her hand.

'You're going to be fine,' she whispered. 'When you come home we're going to take good care of you and the baby.'

'Thank you.'

Lauren squeezed back.

Her hand felt very cold but when Anna kissed her cheek her face felt hot.

Emergency!

'I'm not going to sleep, Auntie Nan,' Casey declared as she snuggled down. 'I'm going to wait until we know about the baby.'

Anna put her arm around her niece and began to read. She'd barely read two pages when she realised Casey had fallen asleep.

Slowly and carefully she moved her arm and kissed Casey's forehead. Her hair lay across the pillow as shiny as a new-minted copper coin and her lashes swept over rosy cheeks dusted with freckles.

Anna felt a surge of love so strong and powerful that it took her breath away.

She realised, if she and Fergus had children, they would probably have red hair, too. The thought pleased her no end.

But Fergus might not want children. It wasn't something they'd ever discussed.

For Anna it wasn't a deal-breaker. All

she wanted in life was to be with Fergus.

She crept downstairs and called him, needing to hear his voice.

'Anna,' he said, replying right away. 'Is everything all right? Why aren't you coming home? Have you changed your mind?'

'Changed my mind about what, Fergus?' she asked. 'About us? Oh, my love, of course I haven't. Don't you know yet how much I love you?'

He let out a relieved little sigh.

'Sorry. I was being silly.'

'You're the least silly person I know,' she replied, 'and I realise this is no way to start our life together, with you at the farm and me at the cottage. The thing is, Lauren's going into hospital.'

'Sorry, I can't hear you,' Fergus said. 'There's a helicopter right overhead. It's really low.

'I can't make out what it is. Perhaps the coastguard or air ambulance. It's heading over the town.'

'I can hear it,' Anna said.

She went to the window and pulled

the curtain back but couldn't see it. All she could hear was the heavy thrum of the rotor blades.

'I hope nothing awful has happened.'

'It may be the police looking for someone,' Fergus mused. 'There's no way of knowing. Anyway, you were telling me about Lauren. The baby isn't due yet, is it?'

'Not for a couple of weeks, but...' She broke off and bit her lip.

'But?'

'I don't know, Fergus. Something didn't seem right. Nick was more worried than I would have expected and Lauren didn't look at all well. He's taken her to the hospital.'

'Shall I come over to be with you?'

'No, no. We'll be fine. I'll let you know when there's any news. I love you, Fergus.'

'I love you, too,' he said. 'With all my heart.'

When she'd hung up, her phone began to ring straight away.

'I've been trying to call you!' Nick

52

said. He sounded desperately worried.

'What's happened?'

'We're about to go in the air ambulance to Stoursley.'

Anna's stomach tightened with fear. Stoursley was a much bigger town on the other side of the estuary. It would take an age to get there by road, so it made sense to send the air ambulance.

'She's not in labour. They think she might have appendicitis and they're just not equipped at our hospital to deal with it!'

'Oh, Nick! What will happen?'

'I wish I knew. She deteriorated suddenly and her temperature has gone through the roof, hence the dash.

'I've got to go. Don't tell Casey!'

'I won't,' she promised. 'I'll be thinking of you both, Nick. Sending all my love.'

He'd already hung up.

Poor Lauren. Poor Nick.

She slumped on the sofa and called Fergus.

'That was quick,' he said cheerfully.

'Do we have a niece or a nephew?'

'Neither. Oh, Fergus!' Anna began to cry as she told him what had happened.

'She'll be all right,' he soothed. 'She's having the best care and they're really good over at Stoursley General. They'll take care of her.'

'I hope you're right. But what am I going to tell Casey?'

'Nothing. By the time she wakes up there may be better news, too.'

Anna didn't go to bed. She couldn't have slept anyway. She paced the floor not knowing what to do with herself.

It wasn't long before there was a soft tap at the door and she hurried to answer it.

'Fergus! What are you doing here?'

'I've come to sit with Casey so you can go and be with Nick,' he explained.

She almost melted with relief. The thought of her brother going through all this worry alone had been tearing her apart.

'What about the farm?'

'Nisha came to the rescue,' he replied.

'I didn't tell her anything except it was a family emergency.'

'That was so kind of her! How did you know I wanted to be with Nick, Fergus?' she whispered as she gathered up her bag and jacket.

'I know you. Promise me you'll drive carefully.'

'I always drive carefully,' she assured him. 'I know I'll be no use to anyone if I end up in a ditch.

'I'll call you when I get there and let you know as soon as there's any news. What will you tell Casey?'

'I'll say you were called out to an emergency. It's not really a lie, is it?'

He hugged her tightly then pushed her away gently.

'You don't have to worry about anything except being with Nick.'

She stared at him for a moment, thinking how very lucky she was and how much she adored him.

'I love you, Fergus.'

She cupped his face in her hands, feeling the softness of his beard against her skin, and kissed him.

Then she ran out to her car, her
thoughts now with Nick and Lauren.

If Only

While Anna was driving through the night to Stoursley Chloe was woken from sleep by Rob's pager.

He sat bolt upright and reached for it.

'Go back to sleep,' he told her as he jumped out of bed and pulled on some clothes.

'Be careful, Rob,' she urged.

He stopped and looked down at her for a moment, frowning.

'I'm always careful.'

He stooped to kiss her goodbye. Chloe longed to hug him but, instead, she turned her face away, hating herself for it all the while.

What if something happened to him? He could be killed and he might die thinking she hated him!

Chloe got up and watched from the window as he drove away through the quiet streets.

If only she could be given the chance to relive the last few minutes so she could have kissed him back and told him she loved him.

'Please be safe,' she whispered as she pressed her cheek against the glass.

Someone out on the water was in trouble and would be delighted to see the lifeboat, Chloe knew very well, but she wouldn't not be able to sleep until she knew he was OK.

As always when Rob was out on a shout she couldn't settle to anything. She made a cup of tea and stood at the window, hoping to see his headlights.

If anything happened to him . . .

Some time later she heard the thrum of a helicopter for the second time in the past few hours.

★ ★ ★

It was starting to get light when his car finally pulled up outside. Chloe was standing at the window, waiting.

All night she had planned how she would run into his arms when he came in, like she used to.

58

Now he was here, safe, the coldness wrapped round her again.

He came in, soaking wet and looking worn out.

'What was it?' she asked.

'A sailor on a small vessel was taken ill,' he explained. 'The sea was pretty rough and none of the guy's family on board knew how to sail the boat.

'We got them back to shore safely and the air ambulance came out to pick the man up. Second time they've been here today.'

'Is he going to be all right?'

'Yes, I think so. I hope so. Right, I'm going to have a shower and get ready for work.'

Chloe nodded.

'I'll get a pot of coffee going and there will be a bacon sandwich ready for you when you come down.'

'Thank you,' he told her. 'I appreciate it.'

Chloe watched him go upstairs, her heart heavy. She made the sandwich and the coffee and left it on the table.

'Come on, Gemma,' she said, rattling the dog's lead.

There was no point staying — Rob wouldn't want her company.

In fact he'd probably just tip his coffee into his travel mug and take his breakfast with him.

Sometimes she felt as if he couldn't bear to be in the same house as her.

Was it any wonder? She was a horrible person.

Traffic Trouble

Lexi manoeuvred the Tiny Tails van down one of the oldest, narrowest streets in Furze Point. The road was cobbled and in better shape than the more modern roads in the town but it could still be quite hairy driving along there, with it being so narrow.

Some of the old houses overhung the pavement below and someone, probably Tom, had told her that the overhang was called a jetty, which seemed a strange name for it.

She was on her way to scan a cat someone had taken in, believing it to be a stray. If they couldn't find the owner she would take it to the vet and then to the rescue for rehoming.

She braked suddenly as she met a car coming the other way. This was awkward. There wasn't room for two vehicles to pass and an unofficial one-way system existed down this particular road.

The council refused to make this

system official but all the locals knew about it. Occasionally a delivery driver would get caught out but that was rare.

The other driver flashed their lights and Lexi flashed her lights back. Two could play at that game!

People stopped to watch what was happening. It was always entertaining when two vehicles met halfway along the road.

Lexi hoped she wouldn't have to reverse all the way down this narrow street. One of them would have to.

The car in front of her was a big, shiny, ink-coloured Mercedes. Her stomach clenched when the driver's door opened and a tall, dark-haired guy got out.

He was definitely not a local. She would have remembered him!

He was very good looking but looked bored and irritated as he approached her van. Now she could see that he was probably only a couple of years older than her. She wondered how he could afford such an expensive car.

She opened her window. Good looks

wouldn't cut any ice with Lexi.

'Could you back up, please?' he asked. 'There isn't room to pass.'

'No. You back up.'

He looked surprised for a moment, as if he wasn't used to being disobeyed, then laughed.

'It'll be easier for you in that little van.'

'No easier than it would be for you in that car. I daresay you have rear cameras and parking sensors so it shouldn't be too difficult for you. Or aren't you any good at reversing?'

'I could ask you the same question,' he retorted. 'If you can just get out of my way I've got an important appointment.'

'So have I!' Lexi replied tartly and closed her window.

She folded her arms, knowing she was in the right here. Sort of.

He looked exasperated then turned to the people watching, spreading his arms in a gesture of hopelessness. If he was hoping for support he was unlucky.

Lexi saw Tom Bennett, the caretaker from Laburnum Villa, step out of the secondhand book store. He waved to Lexi then strolled over.

At the same time Fergus Thompson appeared with Anna's little niece, Casey, holding his hand. He frowned and came over, too.

As always, Tom looked dapper in navy car coat and grey trousers. Fergus was like a mountain in jeans and checked flannel shirt.

It was typical of Fergus not to wear a coat. He didn't seem to feel the cold.

Tom might have been in his sixties but he didn't seem at all fazed or intimidated by the much younger, taller man.

Lexi opened her window again. This was going to be interesting.

'Hello, there,' he began. 'I'm afraid you're going to have to move. You're causing a bit of a traffic jam.'

'That's what I told her,' the younger man said triumphantly.

'I was talking to you,' Tom went on pleasantly. 'As you can see there are two cars behind the van and none behind you, so it's best you move now before

64

things get any worse.'

'If that girl had moved when I told her to this wouldn't have happened!'

The young guy shook his finger in Lexi's direction.

'It's all right, Tom,' Lexi called over. 'I can handle this. I can wait all day if necessary.'

'You must be new around here,' Fergus said, chipping in. 'We have an unofficial one-way system in this road.'

The stranger backed up a little. He looked a little scared.

Lexi smirked, knowing that Fergus wouldn't hurt a fly — he wasn't even bothered by the rats living in his barn, saying every being had the right to live its life in peace.

'No-one told me,' the stranger said sulkily. 'You should put a sign up!'

'We did but the council made us take it down,' Tom said. 'I suggest you take the matter up with them. Perhaps you could persuade them to make it official.'

'I knew it was a mistake moving to this dump!' The stranger scowled at the

65

people watching, all of whom he had just managed to offend.

The people of Furze Point didn't take criticism of their home town lightly!

'The sooner I get away from this hole the better.'

'Hey!' Fergus said, speaking for everyone. 'Steady on. That's our home you're talking about.'

There was a murmur of disgruntled agreement from those watching.

'You're welcome to it!'

He got back in his Mercedes, slammed the door then began to reverse.

'Dump?' Lexi said. 'What a nerve!'

Tom chuckled.

'As I recall you didn't think much of this place yourself when you moved here. Maybe we can bring him round.'

'No, I know a lost cause when I see one,' Lexi said, laughing. 'Thanks anyway, both of you.'

'You're not cross?' Tom asked. 'I know you ladies like to handle things yourselves and I also know you were managing perfectly well.'

'Don't ever apologise for being gallant, Tom,' Lexi told him. 'Do you need a lift anywhere?'

'I'm meeting Carol in the café. Thanks, though.'

'Give Carol my love,' Lexi told him and turned to Fergus. 'Give Anna my love, too.'

It had suddenly occurred to her why Fergus might be looking after Casey. Perhaps the baby was on its way! She was sure it was due around now.

'Hi, Casey. Are you having a lovely time with your uncle Fergus?'

Casey moved closer to Fergus and hugged his hand, gazing up at him with a smile of adoration.

'We're going to get a hot chocolate at the café. Mummy's in the hospital!'

'Well, that's very exciting,' Lexi enthused. 'I bet you can't wait to be a big sister and the baby is going to be very lucky to have you.

'Don't forget to let us know how it goes,' she added to Fergus.

Poor Cat

As Lexi drove on, she saw the Mercedes waiting where the road widened. The driver still looked furious so she gave him a dazzling smile and a cheery wave.

Nothing infuriated an angry person more than having the reason for their anger smile at them!

She went on her way and arrived at a wooden fisherman's cottage down by the old quay. She knocked on the red-painted front door.

'Sorry I'm late, Jean. I got a bit held up.'

'Not a problem. Come in. He's in the back. Is it raining?'

'Trying to!'

Lexi wiped her feet and followed Jean down the hall to the little kitchen where she could see a ragged old ginger cat curled up, fast asleep, on a fat cushion.

'He's not one I recognise,' Jean told her. 'He looks a poor old thing. He appeared a week or so ago.

'He comes in, makes himself at home, has a nap and a bit of fish, then off he goes.

'I keep thinking someone must be missing him — or do you think he's one of those cats with several homes?'

'He's very thin,' Lexi observed. 'Let me just scan for a chip.'

She kneeled down on the floor next to him. As the scanner beeped he opened his eyes and yawned, displaying a full set of white teeth.

'Bingo!'

'Result?'

'Yes, his chip is registered. I'll get in touch with them and see if we can reunite him with his family. His teeth look good and apart from being skinny he seems well looked after.

'What do your other cats think of him?'

'They don't seem to mind him at all,' Jean said. 'I rather hoped . . .'

Her voice tailed away. All Jean's cats were failed fosters in that she took them in until a home could be found and always ended up falling in love with them.

'I'm being silly. He belongs with his family if they can be found.'

'I'll check on the database and see what we can do.'

'Would you like a coffee?'

'You know me!' Lexi said with a smile. 'If I can't trace his owners, I'll put a paper collar on him with my number on it.'

Bad News

When Fergus got home with Casey from their walk he saw Anna's car parked outside the cottage. A thread of cold dread wormed into his chest.

It was going to be good news, bad or no news at all. Anna hadn't called but her phone had been low on charge when she left to drive to Stoursley the night before.

'Auntie Nan!' Casey ran ahead and flung open the little gate, her feet pounding up to the front door.

The door opened and Anna hugged her as the dogs spilled out.

'Where's the baby? Is it here? Where's my mummy?'

'I'm just here to pick up some bits and pieces for Mummy and Daddy,' Anna told her. 'Mummy has to stay in the hospital for a little bit longer and Daddy is going to stay with her.'

'What about the baby? Is it here yet?'

Anna bit her lip.

'You have a little brother, Casey.'

Casey squealed and did a happy dance.

'Is there a photo?'

'Not yet,' Anna said. 'But there will be lots of time for photos.'

She turned to Fergus and looked at the many bags he was carrying.

'You've been shopping!'

'Casey has,' he said with a rueful smile. 'We only went out for a hot chocolate but, as you can see, Casey had other ideas.'

'We bought some things for the baby and for Mummy and Daddy,' Casey explained as she pulled a bright-yellow teddy bear out of one of the bags. 'It's safe for babies. Uncle Fergus made sure. He looked at the labels.'

Anna smiled but it looked a painful one.

'Go in and get your shoes off, then you can show me what you've got and I'll tell you all about baby Caleb.'

'Caleb! Has he got red hair?' Casey said. 'Does he look like me?'

'I haven't seen him yet.'

Anna laughed but Fergus wondered why she hadn't been able to do so.

As soon as Casey had run into the house Anna turned to Fergus.

'I'm not sure about all this.' She nodded at the bags.

'I know,' he apologised. 'She was very insistent and I couldn't say no to her. It seemed to take her mind off worrying.

'Is the news that bad?'

'Lauren had to have emergency surgery for a burst appendix as well as a caesarean section! She and the baby aren't out of the woods yet.

'They're both quite poorly, especially Lauren.'

'Oh, Anna, I'm sorry! I'm an idiot. It was stupid to take Casey shopping.'

'No, don't be sorry. We have to think positive thoughts. To be honest, right now it's Nick I'm fretting about. He didn't sleep all night and he's so worried.

'They told him at the hospital to come home and get some rest but he won't leave Lauren.'

'You didn't sleep, either, did you?'

73

Fergus asked.

'I napped a bit in a chair,' she admitted.

'Do you want to stay here with Casey and I'll drive over to the hospital? I can stay with Nick for as long as he needs me.'

Anna considered, then shook her head.

'It should be me. I'm family.'

'So am I now, Anna,' Fergus reminded her. 'Let me go just for a few hours then we'll swap.'

Anna nodded.

'Thank you. My parents are getting here as soon as they can.'

At the Hospital

Nick was in a corridor, sprawled on the floor fast asleep with a backpack under his head, when Fergus arrived at the hospital.

'Do you know him?' a passing nurse asked. 'See if you can persuade him to go home, will you?'

'I'll try,' Fergus said, 'but I don't hold out much hope.'

Nick jolted awake and stared around for a moment before he looked up. Fergus reached out and pulled Nick to his feet.

'Let me take you home. You need a shower, some food and a proper rest.'

'No! I can't leave her, Fergus. Imagine if it was Anna.' Nick ran his hand across his stubble and shook his head.

Fergus nodded. They'd have to drag him away if it was Anna in the hospital.

'Is there any more news?'

'She's still hanging on. Do you want to see the baby?' There was the slightest spark in Nick's eyes.

'You bet!' Fergus said eagerly.

'They're letting me feed him. They wouldn't even let me hold him at first. He was in shock. It was all a bit . . .'

He shook his head.

'But he's doing better.'

'Is he in an incubator?'

'No. I'll just tell one of the nurses where I'll be in case . . . I mean if . . .'

He stopped at the nurse's station and spoke to someone, then turned and smiled at Fergus. It was an awful smile and Nick looked grey, as if he'd aged ten years or more.

They walked down the corridor and went up in a lift.

'He's on the children's ward,' Nick said. 'There was nowhere else for him. Normally he and Lauren would have been on the maternity ward, but . . .'

Fergus gave Nick's shoulder a squeeze.

'They're both being cared for. That's what matters.'

'He came close to needing to go into PICU but he's been assigned a specialist

76

nurse and they seem pretty happy with him. The birth was very traumatic for him and he was so quiet.

'He was in shock, Fergus! Can you imagine, a little baby born in shock?'

Fergus shook his head. It had to be a good sign that the baby hadn't been put in intensive care, though, didn't it?

The ward was like nothing Fergus had ever seen before. The walls were covered in bright murals and there were toys all down the centre on low tables surrounded by small plastic chairs.

He followed Nick to a cot and looked down at a sleeping baby. The only signs that things weren't as they should be were the presence of a monitor and a drip.

'He looks like Casey!'

Fergus felt a lump form in his throat. The baby was so tiny. He didn't want him to have to grow up without a mother. No wonder Nick was in pieces.

'I've just fed him and got him settled,' a nurse said.

'I'm sorry,' Nick told her. 'I should

have come up but I fell asleep.'

'Why don't you go home and get some rest?' she suggested gently. 'You're not going to be any use to the baby or your wife if you collapse.

She turned to look at Fergus, willing him to agree with her.

'You have a point,' he said, 'but in his shoes I'd want to stay here, too.'

'They're both being looked after,' she said. 'You can take Caleb home tomorrow which will be better for him and for you. Mr Brown is arranging to have the drip removed shortly as he's doing so well.

'You have a strong baby there, Nick.'

Nick looked panicked.

'I don't have anything ready! I don't have my car or the baby seat.'

'Nick,' Fergus said calmly, 'I can sort all that out for you. You should start thinking about coming home.

'Anna and I will help with Caleb and your parents are on their way. You'll have more help than you could possibly need.'

Nick thought, then he nodded.

'Will you go home and bring the car

seat? It's in my car, still parked in the hospital car park at Furze Point,' Nick said as they went back down in the lift.

'We'll get your car,' Fergus replied. 'We can put the seat in Anna's car and she'll come back and pick you and Caleb up.

'But there's no rush. The nurse said tomorrow so I'll stay here awhile and keep you company.'

Nick rubbed at his eyes.

'I should have realised,' he fretted. 'I should have seen something was wrong.'

'Don't start doing that,' Fergus warned. 'You'll drive yourself crazy.'

The lift doors opened and a nurse smiled at them as they stepped out.

'I just sent a message upstairs for you but they said you were on your way down. Lauren's awake and asking for you.'

Nick looked half relieved, half terrified.

'Go!' Fergus urged. 'Be with Lauren. I'll be here.'

He watched Nick race off with the nurse and cuffed away a tear, then called Anna to tell her the good news.

'He'd just taken me to see Caleb,' Fergus said. 'The nurse was waiting when we got out of the lift. You should have seen his face, Anna.'

'I can imagine,' she said. 'Thank you, Fergus. Now he's seen Lauren is OK, see if you can persuade him to come home for a rest, or shall I come over?

'What about the baby? When can he come home? What is he like? I wasn't allowed to see him.'

'Tomorrow,' Fergus said. 'Caleb is coming home tomorrow. He's beautiful, Anna. I said we'd look after him until Lauren is home from hospital.

'I also said that you would drive over to pick Nick and Caleb up. Was that right?'

'Yes, yes it was, Fergus, thank you,' she said. 'I'll get things ready here. Call me when you know what's happening.

'I could bring Casey over to pick the baby up. I think I'll do that once I get the go-ahead.

'Be careful when you do come home won't you, Fergus? Please.'

'I'm always careful,' he replied.

Timmy's Owner

'Tiny Tails,' Lexi said as she answered her phone.

'Are you the person who put a paper collar on my cat?' a woman's voice demanded.

'A very thin ginger cat?' Lexi asked since that was the only one she'd put a collar on.

'He has a medical condition,' the woman replied with an impatient huff. 'He's well looked after! And he's chipped.'

'I'm afraid his microchip details haven't been updated,' Lexi told her. 'Otherwise I would have contacted you.'

Rachel had taught her always to be polite and considerate when speaking to owners, even if they had forgotten something as basic as updating their details — and even if they were furious!

The woman's attitude changed.

'Oh, for goodness sake, I bet he didn't do it! It was one of a list of things I gave my son to do when we moved here.'

She went quiet for a second.

'I'm so sorry! There has been so much to think about but it's unforgivable that Timmy was forgotten. We could have lost him!

'I shall put things right immediately and I will also be having words with my son!'

Lexi softened towards the woman and even felt a pang of sympathy for her son. She clearly thought the world of Timmy.

'What is his medical condition? Hyperthyroidism?'

'Yes. He was so poorly! He'd been losing weight but I thought it was just because he was out and about a lot. He was hungry, though, and occasionally vomiting.

'The vet did blood tests and put him on medication but we haven't got the dosage right yet. I'm considering other measures.'

'Other measures?' If Lexi was a dog her hackles would be rising.

'I've been reading about radioactive iodine therapy. I was going to ask the vet here about it.'

'I see. Well, that's one avenue to explore, though I believe it's very expensive.'

'Timmy's worth it. I'm Angela Chapman, by the way, and I've just taken over the antiques shop in town.

'If you'd care to stop by you can see for yourself that Timmy is loved and cared for. I'd like to make a donation to Tiny Tails as a thank you for being there for him.'

'As it turned out, he didn't need us,' Lexi pointed out.

'Maybe not, but he might have done. Come over when you're free, won't you?

'I'm still setting up the shop so I'm not open yet but if you tap on the window I'll let you in.'

Running Tiny Tails cost a small fortune. Even with the money Lexi and Rachel made from dog grooming and animal hydrotherapy they were always short of cash.

Rachel's partner, Paul, was setting up a ferry service to run between Furze

Point and Stoursley which would hopefully make money one day.

In addition their son, Dominic, always contributed generously when he sold a painting.

'I'll be there when I can,' Lexi promised Angela. 'Thank you. I'll call Jean and let her know that Timmy has a loving home so she won't worry if he visits her.

'I'll tell her not to feed him as well.'

'Thank you. I do have to strictly control his diet so I know what he's getting. Even on the medication if he eats the wrong thing it can upset his poor little tummy.'

'I understand, as will Jean,' Lexi said. 'I look forward to meeting you, Angela.'

Collecting Caleb

Anna found her husband and brother propping each other up on plastic chairs in the corridor. Both were fast asleep, snuggled together like puppies.

She put the baby car seat down on the floor and gazed at them for a moment before gently shaking them awake, smiling at their confused and dazed expressions.

Their red, tired eyes made her heart contract but the smiles on their faces when they saw her were joyous.

'You're here!' Nick said as both men sat up straight. 'Is it time?'

'Not quite. You said Caleb would be discharged at lunchtime, didn't you?'

Nick nodded and licked his dry lips. Anna passed both men a large takeaway coffee.

'I stopped to get those on the way here. I've got you a couple of bacon baps as well, Nick.'

Fergus looked up at her hopefully.

'Two vegetarian sausage baps for you, Fergus,' she added and he beamed.

'Where's Casey?' Nick asked.

Giggling, his little girl stepped out from behind Anna. She was holding a takeaway milkshake.

'Mum and Dad are just getting settled in the cottage, then they're going to come over to see Lauren so you can have a few hours' sleep,' Anna said.

'What about the unit?'

'I've spoken to them. They've got a relief midwife in from here so you don't have to worry about anything. How's Lauren?'

'Doing really well,' he said with a note of pride. 'She's pretty amazing, actually!'

The smile on his face was a soppy one. 'I'm so proud of her.'

'When is Mummy coming home?' Casey asked. 'Why can't she come home now?'

'The doctors and nurses want to make sure she's OK first. She's been poorly but she's much better now.

'I'll ask the nurse if you can come in

86

and see her before we take Caleb home and you can see for yourself.'

Casey nodded furiously.

'She's been brilliant, Daddy,' Anna said. 'So helpful and no trouble at all.'

'I'm not surprised. You're a good girl, Casey. Caleb is very lucky to have you as his big sister.'

'I'm sorry, we can't have so many people here at this time of the day,' an older woman in the dark blue uniform of a senior sister said. 'We don't have all-day visiting. At least two of you will have to leave.'

'I'm waiting to take my baby home,' Nick explained.

'You're not even on the right floor! Why are you cluttering up my corridor?'

'Sister, that's Lauren Novak's husband,' a passing HCA said, making meaningful eyes at the woman.

'Ah. I see. I haven't been on duty for the past few days. Is this your daughter?'

Casey hid behind Fergus.

'Have you come to pick up your little brother?'

'Yes,' Casey squeaked.

'I expect you'd like to see Mummy before you go home. I'll see what I can arrange.'

'Thank you,' Nick said.

'No, I should thank you,' she said sincerely. 'You're Nick Novak, the midwife from Furze Point.

'You delivered my granddaughter two weeks ago under difficult circumstances. My daughter's been singing your praises.

'That apart, you've been through a very difficult time and you look as if you need a shower and twelve hours sleep.'

She looked down at Casey.

'You'll soon be able to see Mummy.'

Casey seemed to see through her brusque exterior and gave Sister a hug.

Nina and George

Chloe walked past Anna's cottage with Gemma. She hadn't heard any news except that Lauren had been whisked off by air ambulance.

There was a car outside and a couple in their fifties emerged from the cottage.

'Have you got everything, George?'

'I don't know,' the man replied tetchily. 'What do I need? I don't even know where we're going.

'I haven't been able to get the satnav to update. The signal round here is terrible!'

He waved the device in the air.

'Let's just get going, George, I don't want to be late. We'll find the way. How difficult can it be?'

Chloe watched as he got in the car. She almost envied them. She and Rob didn't even care enough to bicker any more.

'Stop fiddling with that thing and let's get going,' the woman ordered.

'Good morning!' Chloe called out.

The woman's head popped up from the other side of the car. Chloe thought she looked like an older, female version of Nick while the man had blond hair like Anna.

'Any news?' Chloe asked.

'Mother and baby doing well,' the woman told her. 'Thank you for asking. Are you a friend?'

'Yes, I am,' she replied. 'My name is Chloe.'

'Chloe! You're the one who called Nick, aren't you?'

The woman came round the side of the car.

'I'm Nina, Nick's mum. Thank you! Nick said you may well have saved her life with that phone call.'

'So she's OK?'

Chloe slumped in relief. She'd been in agony wondering what had happened.

'On the mend,' Nina assured her.

'There we go!' George announced from the car. 'I'll just get it to sync with my phone so we can get traffic updates.'

90

Nina rolled her eyes.

'Him and his gadgets. He won't go anywhere without that thing. We could have been halfway there by now!'

'Please give Lauren my love,' Chloe told her.

'We will. Now what, George?'

'The car won't start!' he told her, trying again to turn over the engine. 'It's completely dead.

'How can that be? We drove it all the way from the Lake District!'

Chloe hesitated. She didn't know whether to move on and leave them to it or what to do.

'I'll have to call roadside assistance,' George said as he got out and glared at the car as if it had broken down on purpose.

'Honestly, isn't that typical?' Nina said, then she seemed to notice Gemma for the first time. 'And who is this?'

'Gemma.'

'Hello, Gemma. You're so quiet, I didn't even notice you standing there. Do your children go to the same school as Casey, Chloe?'

'I don't . . .'

'Casey loves it there. She's made so many friends. It was very kind of them to let her take time off during this difficult time and not go on about attendance.'

'She wasn't happy at her last school. They're so much more settled here.'

Chloe realised Nina was talking so much because she was anxious.

'Are they coming?' she asked as George walked over.

'Two hours!' he growled. 'Because this place is quite remote and they are very stretched that's how long we're going to have to wait.'

'Even if they can get here within two hours, there's no guarantee they'll get the car going again.'

'What are we going to do?' Nina cried. 'They're depending on us.'

'I can give you Guy's number,' Chloe offered. 'He runs the local garage. He's very good and very reliable. It may be quicker in the long run.'

'How much is that going to cost?'

George grumbled.

'If you'd just bought a new car when I suggested it instead of insisting on hanging on to this old heap, this would never have happened,' Nina scolded.

'I can take you,' Chloe said. 'I know the way.'

Oh, didn't she just?

All the consultations and procedures she had had done at Stoursley over the years had etched the route indelibly into her brain.

'That's very kind of you but what about getting back?'

'I'm sure something can be arranged. I'll just drop Gemma at home and I'll be right back.'

Baby Blues

On the way back to the house Chloe called Dominic and asked if he'd come in and man the gallery. When she returned George and Nina were waiting anxiously at the roadside.

'You were quick,' Nina said.

'What about my car?' George fretted.

'Don't worry, it's all sorted. We'll drop the keys in to Guy at the garage. He's promised to take a look at it this afternoon.'

'This is so kind of you, Chloe.'

Nina climbed into the back and George sat in the front seat.

'What about fetching your children from school, though?'

'I don't have children,' Chloe said, keeping her eyes firmly on the road.

'I thought you said . . .' Nina began, then stopped. 'You didn't say anything, did you? I just assumed. I'm sorry. Is that by choice?'

'Nina!' George snapped. 'Stop fussing. This is very good of you, Chloe. Anna has always said what a fantastic place this is to live and now Nick says the same.

'It's just a shame they're so far from home.'

'But they're happy, George.'

'So you live in the Lake District,' Chloe said. 'That must be wonderful.'

'The best place in the world although, to hear Anna and Nick talk, you'd think that honour goes to Furze Point.'

Chloe would agree but decided to keep that to herself. She stopped the car outside the garage and George went in with the keys.

'I hope they can get it started before we have to go home,' he said when he reappeared.

'We're staying for a couple of weeks to help Lauren with the baby,' Nina explained.

'No,' George said, 'we're not. I told you I have to get back to work. I can't get any more than a few days off right now.'

'That's just ridiculous! Lauren and Nick need our help. Didn't you tell them that?'

'I did, but I have some important meetings coming up. Deadlines to meet and so on.'

'More important than your own son?'

George sighed. As a distraction Chloe started pointing passing things out to them.

They were both tired and worried. No wonder they were tetchy and bickering.

When they arrived at the hospital and climbed out of the car George put his arm round Nina's shoulders and gave her a tight squeeze.

'They'll be OK,' he said. 'All of them.'

'I know,' Nina replied. 'It's been a very long day, hasn't it? Sorry for snapping, George.'

Chloe bit her lip. How many times should she have told Rob that she was sorry for snapping at him?

Too many to count.

Nina had called ahead to let Nick know they'd arrived and he came out of the hospital now carrying a car seat. He was flanked by Anna and Fergus.

Casey was clutching Fergus's huge hand.

They all spent the next few moments looking at baby Caleb. He was wide awake, regarding them all with slate-blue eyes as if he was sizing them all up. His little mouth smacked contentedly.

Chloe couldn't take her eyes off him. He was so beautiful, so perfect!

'Do you like his yellow bear, Chloe?' Casey demanded. 'I bought it for him.'

'It's beautiful,' she replied. 'He'll treasure that.'

'Mum, Dad, I'll show you to the ward,' Nick said. 'May I leave the baby with you, Anna?'

'I'll come in, too. Casey and Caleb will be all right with Fergus and Chloe. They can be getting them in the car.'

Fergus took the baby carrier as if it weighed nothing at all and Casey slid her hand in Chloe's.

'Where's Rob?' she asked.

'He's at work,' Chloe told her. 'It's just

me, I'm afraid.'

'All on your own?'

Chloe nodded. She thought she might be going to choke on the lump in her throat.

'Are you heading back to town?' Fergus asked as they threaded their way through the packed car park.

'Yes. I can come back for Nina and George if they need a lift.'

'You've already done so much,' Fergus said. 'It's really kind of you, Chloe.'

She watched as Fergus put the car seat in the car carefully, making sure the baby was secure.

'He's so tiny,' he said. 'Look at him.'

Chloe was gazing at him in wonder. He wasn't red or wrinkly even though he'd been born a couple of weeks early. He had closed his little eyes and his mouth formed a little rosebud.

She thought her heart would break as she mourned something she had never had.

Casey looked up at Chloe and squeezed her hand. It was as if she could see right through the smile she'd pasted on to the sadness underneath.

'Can I go home in your car, Chloe?' she wanted to know.

'Oh, er, no, darling. I don't have a child seat in my car. Rob keeps them in his car.'

Because, unlike Rob, she had nothing to do with children.

'That's not a problem,' Fergus told her. 'I can move Casey's seat from this car into yours.'

What could she say?

'I'd love that,' she replied. 'It'll be nice to have company.'

Casey talked non-stop all the way home and Chloe enjoyed listening to her.

She made her laugh, almost made her cry and certainly made the journey seem shorter.

'Can I come and see the paintings?' she asked when Chloe pulled up outside Anna's cottage. 'Mummy says it's not really a place for children.

'I think she thinks I might knock something over or something.'

'Oh, bless you!' Chloe laughed. 'Of course you can. If you like you can spend an afternoon with me at the gallery.'

Casey's eyes went huge.

'Really? Can I? Yes, please, Auntie Chloe!'

Auntie Chloe? Where had that come from?

'Can I call you auntie?' Casey added. 'I always called Mummy's friends that where we used to live.'

'You can call me whatever you like, sweetheart,' Chloe said, suffused with warmth. 'Don't forget, if it's OK with Mummy you can come and spend some time with me.'

'Yes, so I don't have to listen to a baby screaming.' Casey nodded wisely. 'My friend has a baby brother and she said he's always going 'wah-wah-wah'!'

Chloe laughed.

'If it's OK with your parents,' she repeated. She didn't want to overstep. 'We'll have to check with them first.'

Anna's car pulled up behind Chloe and she knew it was time to hand the little girl back to her father.

'Come in and have a coffee, Chloe!' Nick invited.

'I won't, thank you, though. I have to get back to the gallery.'

She bent down and hugged Casey, breathing in the wonderful scent of child. It was a mixture of chocolate and shampoo and pencils.

A strange mix but one that brought the longing within her to the foreground once more.

'We're Married!'

'Was Chloe all right?' Anna asked as Chloe drove off without even saying goodbye.

'I think she was crying,' Casey supplied.

'It's been a very emotional day,' Nick agreed.

They all went into the cottage and Fergus put the kettle on while Nick settled the car seat into an armchair.

Anna's dogs gathered round, quietly looking at the new arrival and gently sniffing the scent of someone new.

'Still asleep,' he pronounced. 'I won't disturb him. Wait, where will Mum and Dad sleep?

'Shall I see if Rosita has any rooms at the Lighthouse?'

'No need,' Anna said. 'It's all sorted out.'

Her heart fluttered. Now was the time.

Fergus came in with some drinks and set them down on the coffee table.

He went to stand beside Anna and slid his arm around her.

'Rosita has space?' Nick queried.

'No need,' Anna said. 'Mum and Dad can have my room. I've got it all ready for them.'

'Where will you sleep, though? You can't sleep on the sofa, even if it is only for a few nights.'

'I was going to tell you before,' Anna replied. 'There has been so much going on.'

'Tell me what?' Nick asked.

His eyes were red and he looked exhausted but there was suddenly a light in them.

'Are you two moving in together?'

'Nick, Fergus and I are married.'

'What?' Nick spluttered, then laughed. 'That's wonderful! I knew you were up to something.

'Did you go to Gretna Green? I bet you had Mum and Dad as witnesses.'

He fired lots of questions but Anna noticed that Casey hadn't said a word. In fact she looked upset.

'What's wrong, sweetie?' Anna asked.

'Everything!' Casey yelled.

Before anyone could stop her she'd run off upstairs, sobbing her heart out.

'I'll go,' Anna told Nick. 'I think Caleb is about to wake up.'

The baby was snuffling and moving his head from side to side. He managed to free a little fist and pressed it against his mouth.

'I'll get him a bottle,' Fergus said.

He saw Nick's doubtful look.

'Don't worry, I'm used to bottle-feeding baby animals. I know about getting the temperature right.'

He winked at Anna.

'There are four bottles in the fridge,' she told him. 'I prepared them earlier.'

She found Casey huddled on her bed, soggy and sobbing.

It had been a difficult few days for the little girl, Anna reasoned. It was hard to remember sometimes just how young she was.

The phrase 'old head on young shoulders' could have been invented for her.

'Casey, sweetie, do you want to talk to me about it? What's wrong? Is something worrying you?'

'Leave me alone!' Casey mumbled into her pillow.

'Please talk to me. You like Fergus, don't you?'

'I love Uncle Fergus!' Casey burst out.

She sat up and glared at Anna. Her face was red and wet and the hurt in her eyes was evident.

'I don't want you to go! I'll miss you!' Casey cried.

She threw her arms round Anna's neck, clinging tightly to her.

'Where will we go? I'm going to miss the dogs, and . . .'

She drew in her breath and the next sentence came out as part of a massive sob.

'I wanted to be your bridesmaid!'

Anna closed her eyes. She should have foreseen this and she was so sorry she hadn't. Still, she was glad it was out in the open.

She got on the bed next to Chloe and

they sat, snuggled up together.

'First of all, I'm only moving to the farm — I won't be hundreds of miles away. I'll come and see you often and you can come up to visit us. OK?'

Casey looked up at her and nodded.

'Secondly, you want to know where you will go. Well, you can stay here if you all want to, for as long as you like.'

'Can we?'

'Of course!'

'What about the dogs?'

Anna bit her lip. This was a tricky one. They were all rescue dogs, bonded and enjoying a settled home life.

She couldn't imagine leaving one or two behind, besides Nick might not want to keep them.

On the other hand her brother loved dogs as much as she did so perhaps a dog of their own was a possibility.

They hadn't been able to have one where they'd lived before but there would be nothing to stop them here.

She couldn't make promises at present.

'I'll bring them to visit and you can visit them, Casey. We can take them for walks together just like we do now.'

'But I'll never be your bridesmaid now!' Casey wailed.

'Of course you will,' Anna assured her. 'We haven't had our wedding reception yet and I'm going to need a bridesmaid at my side for that.

'We'll buy you a lovely dress and . . .'

Anna didn't get the chance to say anything else as Casey was hugging her tightly again.

'You make everything right, Auntie Nan!' she cried.

Anna bit her lip hard. Maybe she had made everything right for Casey but what about Fergus? He had been dead set against a reception or any sort of fuss.

It wouldn't have to be anything big, she reasoned, and Fergus would do anything for Casey.

Somehow Anna would make it work.

New Neighbours

Lexi stopped outside the new façade of the Furze Point Antiques Centre and smiled. There was an elegant chaise longue in the window and, curled up warmly on it, in his very own sunbeam, was Timmy.

Very comfortable he looked, too!

The interior of the shop seemed lovely. Formerly it had been more of a junk shop, but now could be seen some highly polished old furniture and a stunning dining-table upon which Angela was carefully setting out a beautiful old china dinner service.

A Welsh dresser was laden with willow pattern plates and a set of copper jugs in varying sizes.

Lexi tapped on the window and Angela turned round. She was tall, and over her long, red hair she had wound a silk scarf.

She lifted her hand to wave and Lexi saw she was wearing white gloves. As she came towards the door she looked like a

Bohemian model.

Her dress was fitted to a high waist with a full skirt in all shades of yellow and orange. Lexi had never seen anyone quite like her.

Angela's full lips were bright red and her vivid blue eyes were framed by black lashes. She didn't look like the sort of person Lexi had imagined running an antiques shop.

The last owners had been an older couple who used to blend in with the dusty old furniture and odd bits of this and that.

Angela was older than she appeared, Lexi saw from the laughter lines surrounding those blue eyes.

'You must be Lexi,' she said. Her deep, warm voice suited her perfectly. 'Do come in. Would you like a coffee? I was about to take a break.'

Lexi leaned across the chaise and tickled Timmy's ears. He had woken up and yawned when she came in.

'I'd love one, thank you. Timmy looks very much at home.'

'He is! He loves it there, especially when the sun is shining in.

'It's so nice to meet you, Lexi.'

She took off her gloves and offered her hand. Her beautifully manicured finger-nails were painted all different colours.

'I'm Angela, as you already know. We moved into the house next door and we're letting the flat over the shop.

'This is wonderful!' Lexi enthused. 'I love that blue and white china.'

'Spode Blue Italian,' Angela told her. 'Pick it up. Gorgeous, isn't it?'

Carefully Lexi lifted up a plate and studied the design. It was very detailed with a beautiful, peaceful country scene in the centre.

She almost felt she could step into it, speak to the people and pet the sheep.

The edge of the plate was a swirl of flowers and leaves.

'I may start collecting this one day,' Lexi said as she carefully put the plate back.

'As long as you have it out on display and use it,' Angela begged. 'I can't bear

110

it when people buy beautiful things then put them away in boxes, in the hope that they'll gain value.'

'Oh, I would use it!' Lexi agreed.

'There's something so clean about blue and white, isn't there? Now look at this! It's called Spanish Garden and was popular in the 1970s.

'Not really an antique but very pretty. I do love pretty things.'

They went through to the back of the shop and Angela poured two coffees from a coffee-maker. Lexi had half expected an old-fashioned coffee pot and cups and saucers but the mugs were modern.

They sat down at a small, slightly wonky table on a pair of dining-chairs that had seen better days.

'My son is going to do these up,' Angela explained. 'They're nice and sturdy, just not very pretty.

'I still can't quite believe I'm here. It's long been my dream to have my own antiques shop at the seaside.'

She pressed her finger on an envelope and slid it across the table to Lexi.

'For you. Well, for the animals.'

'Thank you. It's very kind of you. May I open it now?'

'Wait till you get back,' Angela said, wrinkling her nose.

Lexi nodded. She didn't know why some people were embarrassed about their donations.

Every little helped. Every single penny was welcome and put to good use.

'Do you know how I started?' Angela asked. 'It was when my mother died. When I cleared her house I found all this old china.

'Some of it had belonged to her grandmother and she'd kept it all those years, packed away in boxes, never seeing the light of day.

'I was going to keep it, too, but Olly, that's my son, said, 'Mum, why don't you sell it?''

She sighed.

'I felt so guilty! I kept wondering what my mother would think. Then I thought, if I don't get rid of it one day it will become Olly's problem.

112

'So I went to see an antiques dealer. I chose poorly. He looked at my mother's treasures and was so dismissive! He offered a few pounds for it and made it sound as if he was doing me a favour by taking it off my hands.

"If that's all it's worth, I may as well keep it,' I told him. I gathered up my china plus my dignity and walked out.

'He called after me, upping his offer a little, but I was having none of it. And neither was he!'

She laughed loudly and Lexi joined in, it was such an infectious, warm laugh.

'I happened to mention it to my hairdresser and she put me in touch with someone who knew about such things.'

Lexi tried not to smile. She really hadn't expected to get Angela's life story!

'Long story short, I took a stall at an antiques fair and sold the lot for far more than that silly man offered me.

'It got me thinking, what if I opened my own shop?'

She dug in a pocket of her skirt and pulled out a tissue.

'Olly's father had died a couple of years before Mum. I thought it would be good to put the money they had left me to good use.

'I started small, opening my little shop at weekends and working as a doctor's receptionist during the week, but my business grew and here I am!

'I have an online presence, too. Olly takes care of that side of things. He's a bit of a geek but don't tell him I said that!'

She leaned forward with a conspiratorial smile.

'He likes to think he's a debonair man-about-town.'

Her face fell a little.

'To me he's still that lost little boy that used to stand at the window waiting for his father to come home. It took him a long time to accept that he'd gone for ever.

'I must admit I was lost for quite a while, too. Finding myself a single parent was daunting.'

'My mother was a single parent,' Lexi

114

told her. 'My dad died when I was two, then Mum died and my sister came home from university to look after me.'

She frowned. She'd never really thought how much Beth had sacrificed for her. For a while, as a teenager, she'd been so ungrateful. Poor Beth.

'Your sister sounds very special.'

'She is. You'll probably meet her — Beth Walsh. She lives at Laburnum Villa.'

'Ah, I've met her husband, Noah.' Angela nodded. 'I booked a chiropractic treatment when we moved in and certainly needed it even though Olly did most of the donkey work.

'Noah and Beth are very lucky to live in such a beautiful place.'

She shook her head.

'Olly was devastated when he realised he'd forgotten to change Timmy's microchip details. In his defence, I did give him a lot to do and he's been working hard, updating the website and shifting stuff.'

There was a yowl as Timmy strolled in.

'Oh, you're awake now, are you?' Angela said. 'You'll be wanting something to eat. I've got you some nice chicken, Timmy.'

To Lexi's surprise Timmy hopped up on her lap and purred loudly as she stroked his soft fur.

'He gave us such a fright when he lost weight. Poor Olly was worried sick — we both were. It was quite a relief to find out it was something treatable.

'We just have to get his medication right now. I've already registered with Marsh Vets and he's booked in there for a blood test.'

'They're very good,' Lexi assured her. 'We always use them. Anna is so nice.'

'So I've heard.' Angela smiled. 'Although I've got an appointment with someone called Willem.'

'Willem De Vries,' Lexi supplied. 'He's the senior partner, originally from the Netherlands and extremely tall. He's a very nice man.

'But I've taken up enough of your time. I'd best be going. I'll come back when you're open. I've already seen something I think my sister would like!'

'Of course.'

Angela lifted Timmy off Lexi's lap.

'You'll get a special discount.'

How lovely it was that someone so nice had moved into Furze Point, Lexi thought as she left. The antiques centre might well bring people into the town.

She hoped they did well.

When she got back to the van she opened the envelope Angela had given her, then gasped.

Rachel was going to be over the moon! The £2000 Angela had donated would pay off a large chunk of their ever-growing vet bill.

Moving Out

It hardly seemed possible that little Caleb Novak was two weeks old already.

Chloe looked down at the baby in her arms, then across to his mother who was curled up on the sofa, fast asleep.

Chloe's gaze returned to the baby. He was so beautiful. His eyes were the bluest blue she'd ever seen and the way he twitched his little mouth made her heart turn over.

'Oh, Chloe!' Lauren sat up and stretched. 'I didn't mean to fall asleep. I'm so sorry.'

'Not a problem,' Chloe said. 'Caleb has been keeping me entertained. Besides, you're still recovering.'

Nick's parents had returned home the week before and had called in to see Chloe at the gallery first, bringing her flowers and thanking her for all her help.

Chloe assured them it was her pleasure and that she'd always be around if Lauren needed her.

She'd called in a few times with shopping and had done a bit of washing for them. Today she'd been passing with Gemma and, seeing that Nick's car wasn't there, had popped in to see if Lauren needed anything.

Nick was meant to be at home but had once again been called into the hospital to do extra shifts.

'It's almost time to get Casey from school,' Lauren said. 'I bet I look a fright.'

'I could get her for you,' Chloe said.

'You've already done enough. What about the gallery?'

'Dominic has stepped in again,' Chloe said, wondering what she would do without him lately. He'd become an almost permanent fixture.

In fact she saw more of him than she did of Rob which was probably just as well.

At times she longed to thaw the frostiness she had created with Rob but it could make it easier when she eventually plucked up the courage to suggest they should part.

He'd probably be relieved.

If only she could just write him a note and leave, but she wouldn't do that to him.

'Come with us,' Lauren said. 'If you want to, that is. Casey would love it if you and Gemma were there to meet her, too. I'll have to tidy myself up and Caleb is due a feed.' She looked at her watch anxiously.

'I could feed him while you get ready.'

'Are you sure? Thank you!'

There was something so special about the weight of the baby in her arms, his warmth and the way he stared at her trustingly as he drank from the bottle.

Lauren had felt the need to explain that she wasn't even going to try to breastfeed after all the problems she had with Casey. She felt sure it contributed to her post-natal depression.

'He's fed, warm and loved,' Chloe had told her. 'That's all that matters.'

When he'd finished Chloe held him against her shoulder and gently rubbed his back until he produced a very loud burp for someone so small.

Lauren came in at that moment and laughed.

'I can see you've done that before,' she said.

'Actually, I haven't,' Chloe replied.

'Well, you're a natural.'

Caleb was asleep when Lauren put him in the pram and they walked together to the school. Chloe couldn't help noticing that Lauren was a little slow and still seemed quite uncomfortable.

'You know I could pick Casey up any time,' she offered. 'If Nick's at work and you're busy with the baby.'

'You're amazing, Chloe,' Lauren said. 'Thank you. I may well take you up on that and I'll let Casey's teacher know.'

Chloe was touched when Casey came out of school and ran straight to her.

'Auntie Chloe! And Gemma!'

'Er, hello?' Lauren said as Casey hugged her, too, before calling one of her friends over to come and look at the beautiful dog.

'You'd think she'd want to show off

her baby brother,' her mother commented with a wry smile. 'But no.'

As Chloe walked home with Casey the little girl held her hand and talked non-stop about her day. While she was with her, Chloe felt uplifted and joyful but as soon as she got back to the gallery and saw Rob waiting inside her heart sank like a stone.

'What are you doing here?' she asked curtly.

'I came to see you.' He squatted down to make a fuss of Gemma. 'I think we need to talk.'

'Not here,' Chloe said.

'It's all right. Dominic's gone home. I said I'd watch the gallery till you got back. We can't go on like this, Chloe.

'I've tried talking to you at home but you open your laptop and say you have urgent work to do or you go off and sit in the bath for two hours.

'I know you're avoiding me. What I don't understand is why.'

She couldn't bear to look at him. Hearing the pain in his voice was bad enough.

'And where do you keep disappearing off to? Dominic said he's been stepping in a lot for you recently. Chloe, are you seeing someone else?'

'I've been helping Lauren with the children, if you must know.'

'Well, that's great! Why didn't you say?' He sounded relieved.

'Because you barely speak to me, plus it's not true that you've tried talking to me. We barely say two words to each other.

'But you're right, something is wrong. I think we should separate.'

She gasped to hear the words she'd gone over and over in her mind.

'Sorry, what? Why?'

'I just don't think it's working,' she said, struggling to keep cool and detached.

'What? We've been together since we were kids, Chloe. I know things aren't right between us but surely we can work it out.'

'Maybe that's the problem,' she replied, seizing on any reason but the real one. 'We've outgrown each other.

I'll move out tonight.'

'Tonight? Where will you go?'

'I'll find somewhere.'

'What about Gemma?'

Chloe looked down at their beloved dog.

'We could go on as we are. She can stay with you at night and come to the gallery with me during the day.'

'You've thought it all through.' He sounded defeated. 'Don't I get a say?'

'The decision is made, Rob.'

'Was it something I did?'

'No.' Her voice almost broke. 'It's not you, it's . . .'

'Don't.' He took a breath. 'Please don't leave me! I love you. There's never been anyone else. Don't you love me any more?'

Of course she loved him. That's why she had to do this.

'Please don't make this any more difficult than it already is.'

It was better this way. Rob could make a fresh start and find someone who could give him the family he deserved.

She was doing it for him.

'Look me in the eye and tell me you don't love me,' Rob said, his voice shaking.

She couldn't look at him let alone reply. 'I'm not giving up on us, Chloe, even if you have. I love you. I will always love you.'

She kept staring down at the polished wooden floor and didn't realise he'd gone until the door closed behind him.

'Oh, Rob,' she cried as the tears she'd been holding back gushed down her face. 'I will always love you, too, but you'll thank me one day. I know you will.'

Party Planning

Anna sat at Beth's big pine table and pushed the list towards her. It was common knowledge that she and Fergus were now married.

'Fergus has agreed to a sort of mini blessing ceremony and a small reception,' she said. 'Purely because Casey wants to be a bridesmaid and he can't say no to her. You know what he's like. I've whittled the list of guests down as much as I can.'

'That's still quite a long list,' Beth said. 'Has Fergus seen it?'

'I'm afraid he'll run a mile if he does,' Anna admitted. 'I don't know what to do, Beth. I don't want to hurt anyone's feelings by not inviting them.'

'Anna, it's your do, you can invite who you like. Everyone knows Fergus and will understand.'

'Well, I want Rosita, Adriana and Jamie to be there and Rob and Chloe, of course. Lexi and Rachel, so Paul and

Dominic, too.

'We'd have to have Tom and Carol, you and Noah. Plus Nick, Lauren and the children.'

'Stop there,' Beth advised. 'That's your guest list.'

'But what about Nisha? She's been so helpful at the farm. Dylan, too.

'Mind you, if I invite Dylan, I'll have to invite everyone else from the surgery.'

'No, you won't. Dylan will be there as Nisha's partner.'

'Oh, they're not partners,' Anna said. 'Just flatmates. They've been friends since school, that's all.'

'That's what they think,' Beth said with a grin.

She went through Anna's list, crossing off names, while Anna watched with a growing sense of relief.

'You have to be ruthless,' Beth declared as she crossed off the last name. 'This is for you and Fergus, no-one else.'

'Except Casey,' Anna said and Beth smiled.

'Except Casey,' she repeated. 'Look,

Anna, I'm having a bit of a party for Lexi for her twenty-first birthday. She doesn't know, of course, but . . .'

'But?'

'I've found our dad! We were told that he'd died but I've found out that he left Mum, that was all. I'm thinking of getting in contact and inviting him along.'

'I wouldn't do that,' Anna warned. 'You could ruin Lexi's birthday!'

'I did wonder about that but I'd like to hear his side of things.'

'You can do that but still, don't invite him to her party without speaking to her first,' Anna advised.

'You're right. I suppose I thought that it would be a wonderful surprise for Lexi but she doesn't really remember him like I do.

'He was such a loving father. I just can't believe he walked out on us without good reason.

'Don't mention it to anyone, will you?'

'Of course I won't.' Anna drew an invisible zip across her lips.

'There will be a surprise party, though,

and I'd love it if you and Fergus came along.'

'As long as that sweet man of mine isn't the centre of attention he'll be fine,' Anna said.

'I'll ask him and Rosita to supply the food,' Beth said with a pleased smile. 'While I'm at it I'll start planning your second wedding.

'Shall we get Rosita to cater that, too?'

'Yes, please. Thank you, Beth.'

The Roadhog

It was the grand opening of the Furze Point Antiques Centre. As Lexi walked, in a glass of Prosecco was placed in her hand.

The shop was packed with people and she smiled as she looked around. She was hoping that Angela made a success of this.

Today she wanted to buy something special for Beth. A small vase caught her eye. It was shaped like a tree trunk with a cute fawn curled up at the base.

It had caught her eye last time she came in.

'That's lovely,' Nisha commented. 'Are you getting it for Beth?'

'How did you guess?'

'It just looks like her sort of thing. Everything's a bit pricey for me, though. Have you seen Angela's son?'

'No, is he here?'

Nisha fanned her face.

'He certainly is. Talk about drop-dead

130

gorgeous!'

'What about Dylan?'

'What about him?' Nisha asked.

'Aren't you and he . . . ?'

Nisha's laugh drew a few looks.

'We're friends, nothing more,' she said, lowering her voice.

At that moment Lexi spotted a familiar face. At first she couldn't place why the face was familiar but then she recognised him as the roadhog who'd made such a fuss about reversing out of her way.

'No,' she whispered.

'That's him!' Nisha said. 'Oliver Chapman, Angela's son.'

Lexi handed Nisha her glass, put the vase down and tried to escape, but the shop was too busy and Angela had spotted her and was calling to her.

She'd seen Angela a couple of times since their first meeting. Timmy's treatment was now going very well and he'd even put on some weight.

Still, she had already met Oliver Chapman and had no desire to speak to him again.

'Come and meet Olly,' Angela called, beckoning her over.

Lexi waved her phone.

'I'm sorry, I've got an emergency,' she fibbed.

Angela didn't hear, just kept waving her over, so Lexi went across.

'Here she is,' Angela said. 'My hero! Olly, meet Lexi.'

Lexi had never before wished so hard that the ground would open up and swallow her. What exactly had she said to him during their encounter?

She couldn't quite remember but was sure she'd been quite rude.

She looked up at him. He was even better looking than she remembered, more so with the big friendly smile on his face.

He held out his hand and gripped hers firmly.

'It's great to meet you at last, Lexi,' he said. 'Mum's always talking about you.'

'I didn't do anything, really.'

'Yes, you did!' Angela protested. 'You

showed an interest, for a start. Besides, if you hadn't helped with that paper collar someone else could have taken Timmy in and we might never have seen him again.'

'True,' Olly said. 'Thank you, Lexi. He means the world to us.'

This man couldn't be all bad if he loved his cat so much, Lexi thought, even if he had forgotten to update his microchip.

'Have we met before?' Olly asked.

She knew from the twinkle in his eyes that he had recognised her.

'I'm sure I would have remembered,' she replied, her cheeks flaming.

'Yes, we did meet,' he insisted. 'My car had broken down and Mum let me borrow hers. I'd never driven it before.'

'He calls it the beast!' Angela laughed. 'It's my one true indulgence — I love it.'

'I was terrified,' Olly went on. 'I knew she'd notice if I got as much as a tiny mark on it.

'I'm used to driving my very basic, very old car while Mum's baby is like a space shuttle!'

'Please excuse me,' Angela said at that point. 'I must mingle. Olly will look after you.'

'Oh, I don't need . . .' Lexi began but the woman had left.

She turned to Angela's son.

'Look, Olly, I'm really sorry about what happened, especially if I was rude.'

'You weren't rude. I admired you, actually. I felt such an idiot, but I was terrified at the thought of reversing back down the road in case I hit something — or someone!

'Come on out the back. I'd love to hear more about your work. You can see Timmy, too.

'He was sleeping peacefully on the chaise but once people started coming in and one lady nearly sat on him he decided to retreat to somewhere quieter and safer.'

New Friends

Olly led her through the back room of the shop and into a small enclosed courtyard filled with potted plants. Apart from the chill in the air you could almost think it was a summer's day.

Timmy was curled up in a pot on some flattened greenery, soaking up the sun.

There were two chairs and a small round table and Olly motioned to Lexi to sit down.

'Can I get you a drink or something to eat?'

'No, thank you.'

'Mum says you do more than just rescue animals,' Olly said.

'I'm training to be a hydrotherapist and I do grooming. It helps to have a source of income. It's very costly running a rescue centre and it's a big old house so you can imagine the upkeep!'

'Is it just the two of you?'

'There's Paul, Rachel and Dominic their son. Paul is setting up a ferry service across to Stoursley and planning to do seal-watching trips.

'You met Paul's dad, actually. Tom was the man who spoke to you that day.'

'Yes, I've met him and Carol since. And the big guy, Fergus. Who's Dominic?'

'He's an artist. A pretty amazing one, actually. What do you do?'

'I run this place with Mum but I also have a workshop nearby. I plan to repair stuff for people and upcycle things people bring in. We never throw anything away.'

'Good to hear.'

'Would you like to see it? It's just round the back of the shops.'

'I'd love to.'

He went over to the back wall and opened a gate. His workshop was a ramshackle old wooden building.

'It's not as fragile as it looks,' he said, seeing the look on her face.

Inside it was packed with interesting things from old individual floor tiles to broken lamps, three-legged tables and chairs with torn upholstery.

There was a box full of broken crockery.

'I'm using this on a table.'

He revealed a round table with pieces of china arranged on the top. Lexi could see he was making a beach scene.

'That's beautiful! I've never seen anything like that before.'

'I don't know what I'll do with it when it's done,' he said. 'Mum only sells genuine articles in the shop. She thinks this is just a hobby, but it's more of a passion.'

'You should ask Chloe to display it in the gallery. It is art, after all.'

'Do you really think she'd be interested?'

She realised that Olly wasn't the arrogant, entitled individual she'd taken him for.

'You can try. She's always open to new ideas and doesn't just display paintings.'

'Thank you,' Olly said. 'I've some other bits and pieces she might be interested in.' He showed Lexi a pair of candlesticks he'd made using old, wooden, cotton-reels and a sparkling decanter he'd turned into a lamp.

'I have to get back,' she said finally. 'I want to buy a gift for my sister first.'

'The vase with the fawn? I saw you looking at it.'

'You were watching me?'

'Hoping to avoid you,' he admitted. 'I'm so embarrassed about what happened. I'm sorry I was such an idiot and said such horrible things about Furze Point. I didn't mean it.'

'We were both at fault.'

'I'd better get back, too. Mum wants me to mingle and meet people. It was good to meet you properly, Lexi.'

'You, too,' she said.

She was buzzing as she went back into the crowded shop. How silly!

Casey's Picture

'Take as long as you like,' Chloe told Nick and Lauren. 'They'll be fine here with me.'

'Don't touch anything, Casey,' Nick said.

Chloe ushered them out of the gallery.

'Go and have fun at the new antiques place. I have your number if I need you and you're only a couple of minutes away.'

Chloe pushed the pram through to her studio and sat Casey at an easel. She had paints and brushes ready for her and, while Chloe fed and changed Caleb, Casey got on with the serious business of painting.

Chloe had often wondered what sort of mother she'd be — whether she'd be like a fish out of water or would take to motherhood naturally.

She knew many didn't find it easy, even those who had longed for a baby.

In the end she found looking after

children suited her very well. She sat in a wicker chair, watching Chloe paint, and imagined how she'd feel if these were her children.

The little girl's brow was furrowed in a frown of concentration.

The baby, fed and clean, gurgled contentedly in her arms. Chloe spoke softly to him and he watched her face, listening to every word.

Occasionally she had to go into the gallery when someone came in and she took him with her.

Casey wore one of Chloe's capes to protect her clothes. Every so often she squealed with frustration and another sheet of paper joined the growing pile in the bin.

At last Caleb's eyes grew heavy and Chloe put him back in his pram to sleep.

'What are you painting, Casey? You've been working on it for a very long time. May I see?'

'Yes!'

She was amazed at the detail Casey had put into the painting. A blazing sun beamed down on a very blue sea which she'd speckled with yellow dots of sunlight.

A yellow sandcastle was in the front of the picture, studded with white shells.

'It's for you,' Casey said. 'It's you and Rob, see? I'm not good at drawing people.'

Chloe looked at the stick figures in the distance. They looked as if they were paddling and were holding hands.

It was so long since she and Rob had held hands or walked together on the beach.

Chloe was sad. She thought everyone must know that she'd left Rob but no-one had told little Casey. Why would they?

'That's lovely, Casey!'

'I've just got to put Gemma in,' Casey said. 'Do you really like it?'

'I do. I love it.'

When she'd finished Casey's dog looked more like a camel and the paint was running where she'd daubed on so much.

'Will you put it up on the wall in the gallery?' she begged.

Chloe almost laughed then realised that Casey was serious.

'Yes,' she said. 'I will. We'll just leave it to dry for now, though. I hope Mummy and Daddy are having a nice time.'

'Is Caleb asleep now? Will you read me a story?'

Casey delved in her backpack and pulled out a book.

'Of course,' Chloe said.

She sat in one of the wicker chairs with Casey on her lap and began to read.

She was so engrossed, she didn't hear someone come into the gallery and had no idea anyone else was there until she looked up and saw Rob standing in the doorway watching her.

Her heart turned over and Casey scrambled off her lap and ran over to him.

'I painted a picture of you and Chloe!' she said. 'Come and see.'

He looked quizzically at Chloe but she looked the other way.

The baby was waking up and she busied herself with him. He just needed a clean nappy and, when she'd settled him again, she realised Rob was still watching her.

'You would make a brilliant mum, Chloe.'

'What did you want, Rob?'

'I just wanted to see if you were OK and if you needed anything.'

Gemma was standing at his side. The poor dog looked lost, as if she didn't know what was happening.

'I'm fine,' she said curtly.

'If it's all right with you I'd like to take Gemma now. I want to have a long walk and she'll be company.'

'Fine.'

'What's wrong with Rob?' Casey asked when he'd left with Gemma.

'Nothing.'

'Yes, there is,' Casey insisted. 'He looked so sad.'

'He's probably just tired,' Chloe replied. 'Shall we finish the story? I want to know what happens!'

'I Found Dad'

Beth peeled away the tissue paper carefully to reveal the vase. Her eyes glistened.

'You bought this for me, Lexi? Why?'

'Because I love you, you idiot,' Lexi said.

'It's beautiful! I'll put it on the dresser.'

'You've still plenty of space for more stuff on there,' Lexi said as Beth put the vase right in the centre of the dresser. 'You should look in the new antiques place.'

'I plan to fill it up as time goes by,' Beth said, 'with special and unusual things.

'Lexi, there's something I need to talk to you about. Sit down.'

Lexi sank into a chair while Beth poured two coffees before returning to the table. The folder she'd seen before was on there.

This wasn't good news . . .

'What is it?' Lexi prompted.

'I don't know where to start,' Beth replied. 'For your twenty-first birthday party I thought it would be nice to make you a family tree so I started researching.'

'Party?' Lexi gave a puzzled smile.

'Yes. It was to be a surprise but in light of what I've found I felt I had to talk to you.'

'Uh-oh!' Lexi laughed. 'What did you find in our past? Murderers?'

'This may be worse,' Beth said. 'Or better. It depends on how you look at it.'

She turned to Lexi and took her hands.

'I found Dad.'

'His grave?'

'No. He's very much alive. I've made contact with him and he wants to come and visit us. I thought perhaps he could be there at your party.'

Lexi jumped to her feet, wrenching her hands from Beth's.

'You mean he abandoned us and Mum? You had to give up your education because of him and we had to move here!'

Beth put her arms round her sister.

'I know what you're feeling because I

felt it, too. I thought of all the years we struggled and the problems when we first moved here. Noah said I should look at it another way, though.'

'What other way? He didn't love us, that much is plain. He has probably looked Laburnum Villa up and thinks you're loaded! That's why he wants to visit.'

Beth shook her head.

'I knew him better than you. He did love us, Lexi, and he has explained why he left.

'There's no point in looking back. If we hadn't moved here I wouldn't have met Noah and you wouldn't be helping to run an animal rescue centre.

'It is what it is, Lexi, and I think we should give him a chance. I was going to invite him to your party as a surprise but Anna said I should warn you first.'

Lexi couldn't think of anything worse. It would spoil everything!

'No way! He has pretended to be dead all those years when we really needed him.'

'It's not that simple. Let me explain.'

'No!' Lexi repeated. 'I'm not interested. He's still dead as far as I'm concerned. Thanks for the coffee but I have to go.'

'Don't go like this. Let me explain.'

'Bye, Beth!'

Lexi ran from the villa and out to the van. Noah called out and waved but she ignored him. She just wanted to get away.

What a thing to find out — that the loving father she thought was dead had just walked out on them, leaving them high and dry.

It was all very well Beth saying they wouldn't have ended up here. It might even be true.

If Mum hadn't been wearing herself out, working so hard for them, however, maybe she wouldn't have been killed. She could still be alive.

As long as she had breath in her body Lexi would never forgive him for that.

Wedding Vows

This was perfect, Fergus thought, looking at the few familiar and dear faces gathered for their second wedding ceremony.

Noah and Rob were at his side, just as he and Rob had been there for Noah when he married Beth.

Beth had done them proud with garlands of flowers in the heated marquee in the grounds of Laburnum Villa. Though this wasn't an official ceremony, Tom was going to say a few words.

It was crazy that they were doing this for one special little girl. Crazy but wonderful.

The music started and Anna appeared with Casey in front of her, scattering petals.

Anna looked stunning in a figure-skimming ivory dress and red flowers woven into her hair.

Casey's red hair was bundled up with white flowers and curls falling around

148

her face. Her dress was sapphire-blue. She'd chosen it herself.

The couple had wanted the day to be as colourful as possible. At Anna's side her brother, Nick, wore a purple shirt and lilac tie with black trousers.

Fergus wore navy-blue trousers and a white-and-green-striped shirt with a bright orange tie.

This was possibly the second-happiest day in Fergus's life, the happiest being the day they'd married in Gretna Green.

Everyone was smiling as Anna joined him and slipped her hand into his.

'Who is giving Anna away?' Tom asked.

'Me!' Nick stepped away to sit down beside Lauren who was cradling the sleeping baby in her arms.

'And who has the important job of holding Anna's flowers?' Tom went on.

'Me!' Casey piped up and stepped forward.

'Thank you, young lady. Well done.'

'I've known Fergus all his life,' Tom told the group. 'I've known Anna for a few years now, too. It is my great pleasure to say a few words today.'

Fergus gave him a look and Tom grinned.

'It will be just a few, I promise! Do you, Fergus, promise to love and care for Anna for ever more?'

'I do.'

'Do you, Anna, promise to love and care for Fergus for ever more?'

'I certainly do.'

'And do you, Casey, promise to love your auntie and uncle for ever more?'

'I do!' Casey shouted.

Everyone laughed.

'Then I am happy to announce that you are now Mr and Mrs Thompson, happily married couple, proud parents to a variety of animals — from feral cats to creaky old horses — and aunt and uncle to Casey and Caleb.'

Casey giggled.

'There is food on the buffet table,' Tom went on. 'Rosita has done us proud, as always, and everything is vegan in Fergus's honour.'

150

Fergus felt his cheeks heat up. He hadn't asked for that!

'It was my idea,' Anna whispered.

'Come on, everybody!' Carol called. 'Enjoy, fill your boots and have a wonderful evening.'

Fergus hugged her. Carol had always been like a surrogate mum and he couldn't love her more if she'd been his flesh and blood.

If he could have planned the perfect wedding — besides the perfect one they'd already had — this would have been it. There was so much laughter and love.

When it was time for the first dance Fergus took Anna in his arms and thought about how close he'd come to losing her and how his life had changed.

He was still the same old Fergus but, for the first time, he knew what it meant to feel complete.

Anna reached up and Fergus lowered his head as she murmured in his ear.

'Have you noticed Rob and Chloe aren't sitting together?'

He looked round.

'I hadn't.'

'Oh, Fergus, something is terribly wrong with those two! They don't even seem to be speaking.

'There's a rumour that Chloe has moved into the Lighthouse. Rosita wouldn't confirm or deny it which makes me think it must be true.'

Fergus froze.

'No,' he said. 'No, that can't be. They're solid, those two!'

'Perhaps you could talk to Rob.'

He shook his head.

'I can't do that. It's none of my business — or anyone else's.'

'I know,' Anna replied. 'But right now he looks as if he needs a friend.'

Fergus considered, then nodded.

'OK, I will, but later. I'll choose my moment.'

Rob is Drunk

The right moment didn't come until later when the evening was coming to a close and the party was winding down.

It was obvious by then that Rob and Chloe were no longer together as they sat as far away from each other as possible.

'We've had a wonderful time,' Lauren told Fergus and Anna. 'You've made a little girl very happy. Casey's had the time of her life. Thank you.'

Casey hugged Fergus and Anna and her smile and rosy cheeks said it all.

It had been worth it, Fergus thought. He'd had a pretty wonderful time himself and that was down to Anna. With her at his side he could do anything.

'We just need to find Caleb!' Nick said, looking round and laughing.

'Chloe's got him,' Lauren said. 'Look.'

They turned and saw Chloe in the corner, the baby cradled in her arms.

She saw them and waved, then got up

and carried Caleb to his parents.

'I don't know what I'd have done without her lately,' Lauren admitted. 'She's been amazing.'

'Are you leaving?' Chloe asked.

'Nick has to be up early tomorrow for his shift. We want to get the children settled, too, although I think this one will be bouncing off the walls all night!'

She ruffled her daughter's hair and the last few flowers fell out.

'I should go now, too.'

Chloe gave a yawn that Fergus thought looked fake.

'Thanks for inviting me. It's been great to see you so happy. I love you both.'

'We love you, too,' Anna told her. 'Do you really have to go?'

'Yes, I think it's best.'

Fergus caught sight of Rob sitting with Noah. He was staring over at Chloe, his eyes dark. Perhaps now would be a good time to have that word.

Just after Chloe left, however, Rob got to his feet and almost fell back into his chair. Noah put a steadying hand on his arm.

Without a word to Anna, Fergus hurried over.

'You all right there, Rob?' he asked.

Noah shot him a look, shaking his head.

'No, I'm not. I'm very much not all right!' Rob spat out.

He wasn't usually much of a drinker and he'd clearly had more than he was used to.

'In case you hadn't noticed Chloe has left me!'

He pushed Noah aside and before anyone could stop him he lurched out of the marquee.

Fergus and Noah followed.

'How can drunk people move so fast?' Noah wondered. 'There he is, with Chloe.'

She was standing beside Rosita's van.

'Go away, Rob,' she was saying. 'You've had too much to drink.'

'Hmm, I wonder why,' Rob countered, putting on a puzzled expression. 'Oh, yes, that's right! My wife left me!

The love of my life decided she didn't love me any more.'

He tapped the top of Rosita's van.

'She would rather live in a bed-and-breakfast than with me.'

'Not here, Rob, please!' Chloe begged. 'This isn't going to change anything.'

'Then where? You won't see me; you won't talk to me. I don't know what to do, Chloe!'

'*I* won't talk to *you*?' Chloe choked. 'That's rich! You're just as bad, Rob.'

Fergus and Noah came up to him.

'Come on, Rob,' Noah urged quietly. 'Let's go back inside. I'll get you a coffee.'

'Coffee?' Rob snarled. 'I don't want coffee! I want my life back the way it was.

'I thought we were happy, Chloe.'

'Is Rosita coming yet?' she asked Fergus. 'Or shall I start walking?'

'Don't walk,' Fergus advised. 'Rob's coming with us. Wait here for Rosita.'

He gripped his friend's arm.

'I'm not going anywhere until I get answers!'

Rob tried to wrench his arm away but Fergus was too strong and, as the fight drained out of him, he slumped helplessly.

'He'll be all right,' Noah told her. 'We'll look after him.'

'I'm so sorry about all this, Fergus,' Chloe whispered.

'Well, I'm sorry you're going through this,' Fergus replied as Noah led Rob away. 'You know where we are if you need to talk to anyone. We're always here for you.'

Rosita, Jamie and Adriana came running out of the marquee.

'What's going on? Chloe, are you all right?'

'I'm fine,' Chloe said. 'Again, I'm so sorry, Fergus. I hope this hasn't ruined your day.'

'Of course not,' he promised and smiled reassuringly. 'We've got this, OK?'

'Look after him,' she begged.

'We will. He'll be fine.'

At the Lighthouse

Chloe felt exhausted after the day's drama but insisted on helping Rosita with washing up and clearing away when they got back to the Lighthouse.

Adriana and Jamie went to bed after much prompting from Rosita. Chloe was certain that it was because she wanted to talk to her.

'Chloe, I . . .' Rosita began.

'I'm sorry about all that unpleasantness back at Laburnum Villa,' Chloe interrupted her as she loaded the dishwasher.

'You don't have anything to apologise for,' Rosita soothed. 'Rob was out of order, acting like that.'

'He didn't mean any harm,' Chloe defended him.

She bit her lip hard to stop herself from crying.

'Rob never gets angry, ever. He's the calmest person I know. It was just the drink.'

'Oh, I know that,' Rosita replied hastily. 'He's a lovely man. I meant that he shouldn't have put you in that position, that's all.

'It's such a shame that you and he . . .'

She broke off and shook her head.

'Sorry, Chloe, I know it's none of my business.'

'These things happen,' Chloe replied. 'Rob will get over it.

'He'll meet someone else who will make him happy, once he gets past this difficult stage.'

'He was already with someone who made him happy,' Rosita pointed out. 'Oh, I'm sorry, I shouldn't have said that.

'I told you when you came to live here that I wouldn't ask questions or pry, and I'll stick to that.

'I just want you to know that, if you ever want to talk, I'm here for you.'

'Thank you,' Chloe said gratefully.

As yet she hadn't told anyone the reason she'd left Rob. She didn't think they'd understand.

'Lauren was singing your praises

during the evening.' Rosita had changed the subject and Chloe's frozen heart softened.

'I enjoy helping them out and those children are just adorable. I love them to bits.'

Rosita smiled.

'I don't think it was easy for Lauren moving here and making a fresh start. She didn't really know anyone except Anna. You've made her feel that she belongs.'

'To be honest it's nice to be able to help someone without them worrying about the fact that I can't have children. It always seems to create awkwardness.

'I don't know if it's real or if I imagine it but it's there all the same. Not with Lauren, though. She just treats me like a friend.'

'It's certain that you can't have children?'

'It would seem so. We've exhausted all out options. We decided not to try IVF any more. It was just too heart-breaking.

'We always had the euphoria of hope

followed by the crash of disappointment.'

'You faced it together, though,' Rosita said gently. 'There are other options.'

Chloe shook her head.

'Not for us. If you don't mind, Rosita, I'd rather not talk about it.'

'I understand, but remember I'm here if you do need to sound off. It won't go any further.'

'I know. Thank you.'

Chloe hugged her. She was so grateful to have such good friends.

She hoped Noah and Fergus would look after Rob. She couldn't bear to think of him being alone and upset.

'I've Lost Her'

The party had broken up and Rob was sitting in Tom and Carol's cottage with his head in his hands.

Noah beside him and Fergus opposite were like two rather large mother hens.

Anna was helping Tom, Carol and Beth to clear up. Fergus knew they were all keeping out of the way.

'I'll be all right now,' Rob told them as he uncovered his face. 'You should get off home, Fergus. I hope I haven't ruined your special day.'

Fergus smiled. Nothing could do that.

'You haven't but we're worried about you, Rob. You're not yourself.'

'I'll be all right,' he repeated. 'Once I figure out why Chloe left me, that is.

'Has she found someone else, do you know? Have you heard anything?'

'As far as we know she's not seeing anyone, Rob,' Noah assured him. 'Did you guys have a row?'

'Not that I can remember.' Rob

frowned. 'Suddenly she just seemed to be really off with me. She stopped fussing about my diet and the importance of keeping fit, for instance, as if she'd given up caring.'

'I don't think she's done that,' Fergus said. 'She was very concerned tonight.'

'If she was so concerned she wouldn't have left me,' Rob argued. 'Part of me feels I should accept her decision and move on but how can I when I love her so much?

'There's never been anyone else for me. I can't imagine a future without Chloe.'

Fergus went to get more coffee. He could hear Noah talking softly to Rob in the other room.

He wondered how he'd feel if Anna left him and realised he'd feel hollowed out, even after their short time as a couple.

Rob and Chloe had been together for years and years. No wonder the poor guy was so bereft! They'd been through so much together, after all.

What would Fergus want people to say to him if he were in Rob's shoes? He didn't know. He couldn't think of anything anyone could say to make him feel better.

In all honesty Fergus would probably prefer to lock himself away at his farm and never see anyone ever again.

'Stay here with us,' Noah was urging Rob when Fergus returned with the coffee. 'Gemma is welcome, too. We've loads of room in the villa.'

Rob was staring at the dog. She was lying on the floor beside Tom and Carol's German Shepherd, Poppy, but she wasn't at all relaxed.

'She's so bewildered,' he said sadly as if he hadn't heard Noah's offer.

It was true, Gemma did look bewildered. She must feel that her life had turned upside down as well.

'You could stay at Bluebell Farm with us,' Fergus suggested.

'I'll be fine. You're not to worry about me.'

'Of course we are going to worry,'

Fergus said. 'We love you.'

'I know.' Rob mustered a small smile. 'I will be OK, though, I promise.

'It's Chloe I'm worried about. She looked so unhappy.'

'You two really need to talk,' Noah advised. 'Thrash this thing out and get to the bottom of it.'

'That's not going to happen,' Rob told him, his voice breaking. 'She's dug her heels in and won't talk to me.

'She thinks there's nothing to talk about and I know I haven't tried hard enough to talk to her.

'I've been scared, to be honest; burying my head in the sand.'

'Lexi's birthday party is coming up,' Noah suggested. 'You'll be invited, of course, and Chloe. You could ask her to dance.'

'And not drink so much next time, mate,' Fergus put in. 'Tonight wasn't like you, Rob.

'Besides, it isn't going to make her any more likely to talk to you if she thinks you're going to make a scene.'

'I know,' Rob conceded unhappily.

'What's the worst that can happen if you do ask her to dance?' Noah asked.

'She can say no and that would be an end to any hope he might have for the future,' Fergus put in.

'She might say yes, though,' Noah countered.

''She can'. 'She might'!' Rob shouted. 'No! I can't do this any more.

'I've lost Chloe. I don't know how or why but that's all there is to it.

'The sooner I get my head around that the better for everyone.'

'Don't give up,' Fergus pleaded. 'Please, Rob. For more than half our lives it's been you and Chloe.'

'Yes, well, maybe it's run its course,' Rob said.

His words sounded so final. It was no longer the drink talking — he seemed to have sobered up.

'For what it's worth I don't think she's fallen out of love with you,' Fergus argued.

'For what it's worth,' Rob echoed his

words, 'it's none of your business!'

'I'll call you a taxi, Rob,' Noah said, casting a sorrowful look at Fergus.

'I'll walk. I need to think.'

He stood up.

'Sorry, guys. I know you're trying to help but this is something I have to sort out on my own.'

'Rob,' Fergus pleaded as his friend headed for the door, 'text me when you get home.'

'OK, Dad,' Rob replied.

There was a hint of the old Rob in his teasing smile.

'What do you think, Fergus?' Noah asked when Rob had left. 'Do you think it's really over for those two?'

'I don't know what to think. I feel guilty that I'm happier than I've ever been in my life while one of my best friends is going through hell.'

'I know the feeling,' Noah responded. 'Don't let it spoil your happiness, though. You deserve this, Fergus. You and Anna both.'

No Time for Romance

'Thanks for coming, Lexi,' Beth said as her sister was leaving. 'We haven't had chance to talk all day but . . .'

'I didn't come here for you,' Lexi said coldly. 'It was for Fergus and Anna.'

'Please don't let's fall out over this,' Beth pleaded. 'I didn't realise it would upset you so much. If it's what you really want I'll tell Dad that I don't want to see him.'

' 'Dad'?' Lexi scoffed.

'You're right to be angry and I understand that, Lexi, I do. You are the most important thing in the world to me and I'm sorry I hurt you.

'I should have spoken to you sooner.'

'Yes, you should.'

'I went about this the wrong way.'

'You certainly did. I have to go. Dominic is on his way to pick me up.'

'Dominic?'

'I was going to get a taxi but he said he'd come back and get me after he took

Rachel and Paul home, that's all.

'So you can stop that right now, Beth. Why would I want to get involved with anyone when my own life is such a mess?'

'Your life is not a mess,' Beth protested.

'Really? My own dad didn't love me enough to stick around so why should I think anyone else would.'

'Oh, love, it wasn't like that. Even if it was I've always been here for you, haven't I? He left me, too, you know.

'I'm so sorry. The last thing I want to do is upset you.'

'Would you break contact with our father for me?' Lexi challenged.

'Yes. I'd do anything for you, Lexi, you know that.'

'Why did he leave us, Beth? What did we do?' Lexi whispered.

'He was having an affair,' Beth said sadly. 'Mum found out and told him to leave.

'He promised to break it off but Mum said she'd never be able to trust him again. You know what she was like.'

'Yes, she was fiercely protective over us!' Lexi defended her. 'She deserved better.'

'Anyway, Mum told him that he was dead to us and should stay that way. When he sent money she returned it to him.

'I don't know who else knew the truth.'

'Did he marry this other woman?' Lexi asked, curious.

Beth shook her head.

'He's on his own. I think he's very aware of how much he lost. When he found out Mum had died he broke down and cried.'

'How would you feel if Noah cheated on you?' Lexi wanted to know.

Beth flinched.

'I honestly don't know.'

Dominic's car pulled into the car park and Carol appeared. She ran over to say hello to her grandson.

'I'd better go,' Lexi said.

'Are we friends, Lexi?'

'Of course.'

How could she stay cross with her

sister after all they'd been through?

'Are you still OK with me arranging your birthday party?'

'I wouldn't have anyone else do it. We don't need anyone else, either. We certainly don't need that man in our lives.'

Beth nodded.

'I'll explain that to him.'

'Good. Blame me, I don't care.'

She got into the car beside Dominic and breathed a sigh of relief as he pulled away.

'Have you and Beth made up?' he asked. 'I noticed during the evening that you were barely speaking. It's not like you.'

'Yes. It was all nothing, really.'

'Good. Oh, Oliver Chapman called just after I got home with Mum and Dad.'

'Who?' Lexi was glad it was dark so that Dominic wouldn't see her blush.

It hadn't slipped her notice, though, that Dominic had referred to Rachel and Paul as Mum and Dad. They were, of course, but he hadn't known them all that long.

'The guy from the antiques place — Timmy's owner. He said he'd been trying your mobile but you weren't answering.'

'Oh, him. What did he want?'

'He wanted to talk to you about re-homing a dog. Apparently Timmy loves dogs and he thought you might be able to help him find a perfect match.'

'He could have spoken to Rachel.' Dominic sniffed.

'Well, he specifically asked for you. I said you'd meet him at the Lighthouse for coffee on Thursday at eleven.

'I checked your diary; you're free then.'

'I'll be pleased to see him if he's serious about rehoming.'

'Is that the only reason?' Dominic asked, his voice gruff.

She was amazed that Dominic would even care, not that there was anything to care about.

Romance was the last thing on Lexi's agenda. She was far too busy for all that and, besides, what she'd told Beth was entirely true.

Fearful

Lauren stood outside the gallery looking in. Chloe was at the desk in the centre, not doing anything, just staring into space. She looked tortured and exhausted.

Lauren felt ashamed over how heavily she'd leaned on her new friend these past few weeks while she was recovering. Now she was well again it was time to return the favour — if she knew how.

Certainly it wasn't fair to use Chloe as an unpaid babysitter. Lauren had lost count of how often she'd asked Chloe to pick Casey up from school or watch the baby.

It wasn't just that. Everyone knew that Chloe had left her husband. What sort of friend would Lauren be if she didn't speak to her about it?

To herself she admitted that at the back of her mind was a fear that Chloe was trying to take over. She was sure Chloe had no intention of doing so but even the fact that the thought was there frightened her.

It was how she'd felt after Casey was born and it had overwhelmed her. She'd become convinced that they — whoever they were — planned to take Casey away.

Thank goodness for Nick and his support, also their wonderful doctor who had diagnosed post-natal depression.

She pushed the gallery door open. Chloe came out of her trance with a start.

'Lauren! Where are the children?' she asked, concerned.

'They're with Nick.'

Chloe slumped back with a relieved sigh.

'You don't have to worry about them. They're not your responsibility.'

Chloe's eyes hardened.

'I know that!'

'Sorry, I didn't mean it to come out like that. Do you want to shut up shop and come for a coffee?'

'I can't.'

'I guessed you'd say that.' Lauren held up a bag. 'I bought these.'

'What are they?'

174

'Just two of the best cream slices that Furze Point Bakery has to offer!' Lauren said. 'I also picked up a chewy stick for Gemma.'

She bent to stroke the dog who wagged her tail, having already smelled her treat.

'Yes, I did!' she said. 'A treat for a special girl!

'Oh, we really have to get a dog. Casey misses Anna's dogs so much and I do think children should be brought up with animals. I'll wait until spring or summer, I think.'

'Come through to the studio,' Chloe said. 'I'll put the kettle on and prop the door open so I'll hear if anyone comes in.'

Lauren stopped dead in front of a painting in a prominent position on the wall.

'What's this?'

'My favourite piece by my favourite young artist. A lot of people have admired it. They're amazed when I tell them it's the work of a five-year-old!'

Lauren nodded.

'I assume it's one of Casey's and it

looks like a perfect day at the beach, but it's just a child's picture. Why is it here amongst all these beautiful, professional works?'

'Because I promised Casey I'd put it on the wall and I can't see it without smiling — it brightens my day.

'She has talent. I'm sure that, one day, she'll be an artist if that's what she wants.'

'Who are the figures? Nick and me? Oh, wait, there's a dog. It's you, Rob and Gemma!'

Lauren saw tears shimmer in Chloe's eyes which she quickly brushed away.

'Thank you for putting it on the wall,' she said gently. 'It will mean the world to Casey. I'll bring her in so she can see it.

'She enjoyed her time here with you.'

'She's always welcome.'

Lauren looked around the studio.

'What are you working on at the moment?'

'A personal project.' Chloe looked embarrassed. 'It's not finished but it's a gift for you and Nick.'

She turned an easel around and Lauren gasped as she saw her own likeness as well as Nick and their children.

It was a family portrait, something Lauren had always wanted but could never afford.

'It's beautiful! You've made me look, well, radiant.'

'It's how you look to me,' Chloe explained. 'Motherhood brings something out in you. A light.'

'Thank you. As for Nick, you've captured his strength and softness. Casey's mischievousness is there and even Caleb has a light about him.

'This is truly amazing, Chloe. Thank you.'

She turned to hug her friend.

'I've seen that radiance in you when you hold Caleb or play with Casey,' she told her. 'It's not just motherhood, it's love.'

Chloe tried to laugh but her laughter turned into sobs.

Lauren held her tightly. She'd said the wrong thing!

'We're Finished'

In the end it was Lauren who put the kettle on while Chloe composed herself.

They sat in wicker chairs in a beam of sunlight. Chloe stared past Lauren.

'Has anyone told you about me?' she asked.

'That you've left Rob and moved into the Lighthouse? Yes, I know about that. If you want to talk about it I'm here for you.'

'Did they say why I left him?'

'I don't think anyone knows,' Lauren replied. 'What I've heard isn't gossip, though. It's concern. People are worried about you both.'

'We've been trying for a family for years,' Chloe explained. 'I've had tests, treatments, IVF, special diets, you name it. They don't know why I can't conceive.

'One doctor even told me to stop worrying about it and it might happen. As if it's as easy as that!'

'I had no idea,' Lauren said. Guilt

rose within her. 'If I'd known I would never . . .'

'Never have asked me to help out with Casey and Caleb?' Chloe finished. 'I know but that's what I've loved about our friendship.

'You haven't been treading on egg-shells around me.'

'It goes both ways,' Lauren urged. 'You know nothing of the post-natal depression I had after Casey was born — how I struggled and was convinced that I'd be declared an unfit mother and she'd be taken away from me.'

'Oh, Lauren, I had no idea!'

Lauren grasped Chloe's hands.

'We mustn't let any of this affect our friendship. It should make it stronger.

'Talk to me, Chloe. You've helped me all this time so now it's my turn to try to help you.'

'Well, you've seen how Rob is round kids,' Chloe said. 'He's a natural. I just feel he needs to be with someone who can give him the family he wants.'

'I've seen you around kids, too,'

Lauren argued. 'You'd make a wonderful mother.'

'Don't!' Chloe cried. 'Rob doesn't know that's why I left him. You mustn't tell anyone.'

'I won't, of course, but why didn't you tell him yourself?'

'He wouldn't understand.'

'There are other options,' Lauren suggested. 'Have you considered adoption?'

'It wouldn't be the same.' Chloe shook her head. 'And what if we weren't accepted? It would mean more disappointment. It isn't easy to adopt.'

'Nor should it be,' Lauren agreed. 'Don't you think it would be worth it for you and for the child, though?

'I know you have so much love to give because of how you are with Casey and Caleb. They love you, too. Caleb isn't as calm for anyone as he is for you!

'Talk to Rob, Chloe. Tell him what you have told me.'

Chloe thought.

'I'll try,' she said finally.

'Remember, *you* are Rob's family. You

and Gemma. I know that's easy for me to say but it's true.

'I'm certain he'd rather be with you, and only you, than with anyone else and have half a dozen kids.'

'Do you think I'm silly?'

'Not at all. You're hurt and upset and sometimes things just become too much.

'The one person you should be able to talk to is Rob. He'll understand, I promise you.'

Chloe stood up and made more coffee.

'Thank you for coming today, Lauren,' she said. 'Thank you, too, for letting me be a part of your lovely family.

'You're just so perfect. The sort of family I always longed for.'

'We're not perfect, Chloe. I didn't bond with Casey straight away and I was terrified she'd be taken away from me, as I said.

'I thought Nick might leave me and I treated him horribly. Thank goodness he realised what was wrong and got me the help I needed!'

'That must have been difficult.'

'It was but we got through it. I've been so afraid the same thing would happen this time but I think we're going to be fine.'

'I know you are,' Chloe said.

They heard the door to the gallery open and close. Chloe hurried out to see who it was.

'Rob!'

Lauren heard that. If only there was another way out of the gallery! The studio just opened out into a courtyard garden.

'Have you got a minute?'

Gemma's claws tapped across the floor as she heard Rob's voice and hurried out to greet him.

'Yes, of course. Actually I was going to get in touch.'

'Good. It's just, I was thinking maybe we should put the house on the market. It's ridiculous for me to go on living there.

'It's taken me a while but I've finally come to terms with what's happening.'

Lauren put her hands over her mouth. Oh, no, not now! Not when Chloe had decided to talk to him!

She closed her eyes.

'Tell him, Chloe,' she whispered. 'Tell him you love him.'

'I don't know why you've fallen out of love with me,' Rob went on as Chloe stayed silent. 'Maybe I wasn't supportive or understanding enough.

'It's happened, though, and I realise we have to move on. You can't go on living in a B and B, even if it is Rosita's.'

'Say something, Chloe!' Lauren begged.

Still Chloe said nothing.

'Anyway, I'll leave you to think about it. One more thing. I really hope we can remain friends. It'll make things easier.

'Bye, Chloe.'

The door opened and closed again.

Lauren rushed into the gallery where Chloe stood, her face bleached of colour.

'Did you hear?'

'I did. Why didn't you say something?

You just let him talk.'

'What could I say?' Chloe gave a miserable shrug. 'It proves I was right. We really are finished.'

Perfect Match

'Hi, Olly,' Lexi said as she took a seat at the table opposite Oliver Chapman.

He jumped to his feet.

'Lexi! I didn't see you coming.' He smiled and sat down again.

How had she ever thought him arrogant? He seemed almost shy and rather nervous.

Rosita came over and took their order. She winked at Lexi before hurrying off.

Olly waved his hand towards the water shimmering in the sun.

'I thought my mother was mad, wanting to move here,' he marvelled.

'To this dump, you mean?' she teased.

'Sorry about that. It was hard to leave my friends behind and the life I was building for myself. I acted like a spoiled brat.'

'I know how that feels. I played my sister Beth up so much when we moved here!'

'Mum said I should come and give it a

185

year to see how I felt. She'd never asked me for anything before so I agreed.

'Now I see this place has a lot to offer. I'm thinking of learning how to sail.'

'It took me longer than that to see how special this place is. Mind you, it's not always this calm. It can be wild in a gale!'

Rosita brought their coffee and cakes as Lexi showed Olly pictures of some of the dogs and cats in their care.

'These cats can all be homed with another calm cat and we have three dogs who are cat-tested.

'If you decide on any there will have to be careful introductions but we can help.

'One thing. If you plan to leave after a year what will happen to the animal?'

'You think of everything, don't you?'

'We have to.'

Olly nodded.

'I guess I would probably have to leave it here with Mum and Timmy.'

'Thanks for your honesty,' Lexi told him. 'I'll speak to your mother and to Rachel about your situation. In the meantime, how do you fancy coming to a party?'

'Now you're talking!' he said with a grin.

'It's my twenty-first birthday party at Laburnum Villa. It nearly got cancelled.'

'Why?'

'I thought our dad was dead,' she said bluntly. 'Turns out he just left when I was a baby. Now my sister has found him and tells me she wanted to invite him to my party!

'I said no, naturally!'

She waited for him to agree with her but he frowned and shook his head.

'You think I'm wrong?'

'My dad did die,' Olly explained. 'All I know is that I would give anything to see him again. If I found out he was still alive I'd be over the moon.'

'Even if he'd deserted you?'

'He'd still be my dad.' Olly shrugged. 'I'd want to give him a chance, at least.'

Lexi stood up, irritated. It was clear she wouldn't get any sympathy from Olly.

'Thanks for the coffee. I'll be in touch and we'll arrange for you to come to Tiny Tails so you can meet some of the animals.'

'Hey, I'm sorry if that wasn't the right answer,' he said. 'I was being truthful.'

'I know. Thanks, and I still want you to come to the party. It'll be a good chance for you to meet more people.'

'I'd love to,' he told her. 'Thank you.'

'Bring your mum!' Lexi called back. 'The more the merrier. I'll make sure Beth sends you an invitation.'

★ ★ ★

Olly and Angela sat in Rachel's sitting-room, nervous. This was their third visit to Tiny Tails. Last time they'd taken Midge, an untidy little grey terrier-type dog, for a short walk round the exercise area.

If he got on with Timmy then he'd be staying with them.

The moment he came into the room and saw them he began to wag his tail, rushing from one to the other of them.

'I think that confirms it,' Lexi told them, smiling. 'He's definitely chosen you. Are you happy to proceed?'

Midge was up on Angela's lap, licking her face.

'He's gorgeous!' she said. 'I already love him so much. Yes, we're very happy, aren't we, Olly?'

'Absolutely. I can't wait to take him home and start taking him for walks.'

'You're happy about introducing him gradually to Timmy? He's been tested and is well behaved around cats. You said Timmy never runs from a dog.'

'We'll keep him on a lead when he's near Timmy at first,' Angela vowed. 'See how we go from there. I promise we'll take good care of him, Lexi.'

'I know you will.'

Rachel came into the room.

'This looks like a match made in heaven,' she said, laughing. 'You're a very lucky boy, Midge. Any problems at all we're here to help. Don't be afraid to ask.'

'We won't,' Olly said. 'Be afraid to ask, I mean!'

Angela took a harness out of her bag and slipped it on Midge.

'I've got a collar with his name and contact details on, too,' she informed them. 'There's a seatbelt for him in the car but Olly will sit in the back with him anyway.'

Lexi walked with them to the Mercedes and watched as Midge hopped inside without a backward glance.

Olly climbed in beside the little dog.

'I hope you'll be very happy,' Lexi told them.

'We will,' Angela replied. 'If Olly leaves it'll be easier if I have company, too. Midge will give me a reason to go out every day.'

'You think Olly will leave?'

'It's always possible, isn't it?' his mother said. 'If there's one thing that's certain in this life it's that nothing is certain!

'Oh, I must get a dog-gate for the front door of the shop. I'll keep Midge in there

190

with me if he's not in the workshop with Olly. I won't risk him running off.'

Looking at how happy Midge looked with his new family Lexi couldn't see that ever happening!

Here was a dog who knew he had found his for ever home, if ever she'd seen one!

Memories

A few days later Chloe spotted the 'For Sale' sign in the front garden of her house.

She hurried to the front door and let herself in. Gemma rushed to greet her and she looked round the house that was no longer her home.

There was a note on the kitchen table.

Put stickers on everything you want to keep. I'll see to the rest.

'Oh, Gemma, what have I done?' Chloe cried and fell to her knees, burying her face in the Labrador's soft fur.

'The right thing,' the voice in her head assured her. 'This proves it was what he wanted all along.'

She went from room to room. It all seemed so empty. Rob was keeping it tidy but there was nothing of home about it.

There were still pictures of them on the sideboard and stuck to the fridge. They looked so young and happy in the photos.

She took one off the fridge then put it back. What was the point in hanging on to anything from the past?

She wrote on the bottom of Rob's note. *I don't want any of it.*

Anything she took from the house would only serve as a reminder of what she'd lost.

She hurried out with Gemma and headed for the gallery. Later, as always, she'd take her home before Rob got back from work. Their paths never had to cross and if they had to communicate at all, they did it via notes on the kitchen table.

Chloe just hoped wherever he moved that she'd still be able to share Gemma's care. She couldn't bear to lose her, too.

When she arrived at the gallery a pink envelope had been put through the door. It was an invitation to Lexi's twenty-first and she'd added a postscript. *Bring Gemma!*

Chloe would love to go to the party, but how could she? What if Rob had already met someone and brought her or she had to watch him dancing with other women?

Rob wouldn't set out to hurt her, but she had to face it. It had been her plan all along for him to make a fresh start. She mustn't be upset if he was doing just that.

Dominic came into the gallery behind her.

'You got an invitation, then? I think they're asking half the town!'

'It'll be lovely,' Chloe replied. 'What have you got? Something new for me?'

'It's not a seascape,' he warned. 'I wanted to try something different. I took a couple of the Tiny Tails dogs for a walk in the woods behind Bluebell Farm and the light was amazing, soft and ethereal.

'I went back and, luckily for me, the weather held for a few days.'

He uncovered the picture and Chloe gasped. He had captured it perfectly. She felt she could go into the painting and feel the healing aura of the trees.

'You don't like it?' he asked uncertainly.

'I love it! It'll be snapped up.'

She caught sight of someone walking past and waved. Dominic turned and waved, too, beckoning for him to come in.

'You have to meet Olly's new dog,' he told her. 'Lexi paired them up.'

Olly opened the door.

'Is it OK to bring Midge in?'

Chloe clapped her hands when she saw the little dog, an untidy fringe almost covering his bright brown eyes.

'Of course! He's lovely. Hello, Midge.'

The dog greeted her and Dominic then approached Gemma and went down on his elbows, bottom in the air, tail wagging.

'He wants to play. Does he get on with your cat?'

'Well, he already knows that Timmy is the boss. They haven't curled up together yet, but they sleep at opposite ends of the sofa. I think they're going to get along just fine.

'Is that an invitation to the party? I got one, too. I'm looking forward to it. Lexi's the first real friend I've made here.'

Dominic made a strange choking sound. 'I've got stuff to do out the back,' he muttered and headed towards the studio.

'I'll go as well. I promised this one a walk on the beach.

'I would have taken all the dogs from Tiny Tails if I could but there was something special about Midge. We just clicked.'

'It was like that when we got Gemma,' Chloe recalled. 'She'd had two homes before she came to us.

'I wondered if she'd settle but on the very first day she climbed up on Rob's lap and we knew she'd be happy with us.'

As she spoke she thought of everything she'd left behind at the house.

There was nothing she could do about her memories. They would be there to torture her for ever.

When Olly had gone, she looked again at the invitation.

She would have to attend. All her friends would be there and, besides, she didn't want to let Lexi down.

Good News

Lexi found her sister out the back, helping Marie with the horses.

'I'll come back if you're busy,' she said.

'Never too busy to talk to you,' Beth said. 'What's up?'

'It's about the party. I've had a few days to think and I've changed my mind.'

'What? Oh, no! I've sent all the invitations out, I've got the food ordered from Rosita and Fergus is supplying all the salads!'

'Not about the party.' Lexi laughed, rolling her eyes. 'I mean about inviting our father. I'd like to meet him first and, if that goes well, then he can come to the party.'

'Really? You're OK with that? Lexi, this is your party and you don't have to do anything you don't want to do.

'I've already explained to him that he won't be welcome.'

Lexi could see that Beth was trying not to look delighted with her change of heart.

'What made you change your mind?'

'Something Olly said the other day,' Lexi admitted. 'His dad did die and he says he'd give anything to see him again. I realised I'm lucky to have the chance to see him.'

'Olly's right. Dad made mistakes but we all do, don't we? So, Olly?'

'Stop that.' Lexi smiled. 'He's a nice guy in the same way Dominic is a nice guy.

'I'm too busy for romance. Look how old you were when you met Noah!'

'Ancient!' Beth laughed. 'But it's good to see you happy and settled. You are happy, aren't you?'

'Happier than I've been for a very long time. Did you really tell Dad he wouldn't be welcome?'

'Not in those words. I said perhaps we should leave any meetings for a while, that's all. I hoped you'd come round.'

'You know me so well!'

'I've some news that might make you even happier,' Beth said. 'How do you feel about being an aunt?'

'In what way?' Lexi asked.

'In the way of me having a baby.'

'Oh, I wish you both all the luck in the world. Have you been trying long? Wait, don't answer that. It's none of my business.

'When are you planning it?'

'In about six months,' Beth replied with a smile.

'How? Are you adopting?'

Beth laughed and hugged her sister.

'I'm pregnant, you goose!'

'What? That's wonderful news!'

Lexi jumped up and down. She was going to be an aunt! Her family was getting bigger and bigger.

'Congratulations! I bet Noah is over the moon. Why didn't you tell me sooner?

'Do you know what sex it is? Do you want to know?'

She realised that Beth was no longer smiling.

'Did I say something wrong?'

'No, love. We haven't told anyone yet. Partly because we were waiting for a scan to confirm everything is OK but mostly because of Chloe.'

'Chloe?'

'It seems unfair, that's all. She and Rob tried for years to have a baby and it's happened straight away for us.'

Lexi shook her head.

'You mustn't think like that. You have every right to be happy. Chloe will understand.'

'I just feel so sad for her,' Beth said tearfully. 'Sorry I'm crying. It's hormones, apparently.

'I can't believe Chloe and Rob have split up! They always seemed so together and steady. You start to think, if it can happen to them, it could happen to any of us. Nothing in life is certain.'

Lexi took Beth's hands and pressed them against her still-flat stomach.

'You have a little baby in there. I don't know much about pregnancy but I do know it's good to think happy thoughts.

'Chloe will be hurt if you don't tell her the news. Does anyone else know?'

'Nick saw us up at the maternity unit

when we went for a scan. He won't tell anyone but people will have seen us at the hospital. You know how things get round.'

'Then you must tell Chloe as soon as possible. Let her be part of this, Beth. Don't make her feel that your friendship will change. Look what a good friend she's been to Lauren.'

'We could ask her and Rob to be godparents,' Beth mused, then frowned. 'Would that be rubbing it in, though? Oh, I don't know what to do.'

'Trust yourself,' Lexi advised. 'You're a lovely person, much as it pains me to admit it, bossy big sister!

'Don't start by being odd about it, though. Share the news like you would any other. It'll only be weird if you make it so.'

'You're very wise for someone so young,' Beth told her.

'I take after my sister,' Lexi said, 'when she isn't suffering from pregnancy brain.'

Catch Up

Chloe saw Beth walking towards her along the beach with her Dalmatian, Pongo. As soon as he saw Gemma he came bounding towards them.

Chloe laughed as Gemma braced herself, then burst into life and chased Pongo along the shore.

'Hey, Chloe!' Beth said. 'Just the person I wanted to see. It's been ages since we had a proper get-together.

'Do you fancy coming up to the villa for a coffee and catch up?'

Chloe tried to think of an excuse not to go. No doubt Beth wanted to talk to her about Rob and she really didn't want to discuss it.

'I've got some exciting news I want to share,' Beth said. 'Well, two bits of exciting news, actually.

'You are coming to Lexi's birthday party, aren't you?'

She linked her arm through Chloe's and they walked together along the beach while the dogs charged up and down getting muddy, sandy and soaking wet.

'I was going to call by the gallery but this is even better,' Beth explained. 'Is Dominic looking after things there? How's it going with him?'

'I don't think I should come back to yours,' Chloe prevaricated. 'Look at the mess Gemma is in.'

Beth waved her hand.

'No worse than Pongo! We can hose them down in the yard and dry them off with towels, then I'll run you back to the gallery later.

'How does that sound?'

'Great. So, what's your news?'

'First, I've found my dad!' Beth said.

'Your dad? I thought he'd died!'

'So did I, but it turns out he didn't. He and Mum split up and for various reasons he had to step away.

'He didn't even know Mum had passed away. He was devastated when I told him. I really think that, despite everything, she was the love of his life.'

'How do you feel about this, Beth?'

'I just want to see him. He was a lovely father. Lexi doesn't remember him like I do and she's not quite so keen.

'Still, she's agreed that he should meet her and maybe come to her birthday party.'

'That's amazing!'

'It is, isn't it? Especially now.'

They turned up the path to the villa and called the dogs. Beth went to get towels while Chloe started hosing the mud and sand off the dogs' fur.

They pranced about thinking it was a great game and both shook, soaking Chloe in the process.

She was in fits of laughter when Beth returned.

'You've sand in your hair,' Beth pointed out. 'Should I hose you down, too?'

'I'll pass, thanks!' Chloe laughed.

Gemma and Pongo loved being rubbed with the towels. When they went into Beth's kitchen the dogs lay down together in front of the Aga.

'I'm having a hot chocolate to warm

myself up,' Beth said. 'Fancy the same or would you prefer coffee?'

'I haven't had hot chocolate for ages,' Chloe replied. 'I'd love one.'

She watched as Beth made the drinks and thought how well she looked.

Glowing, in fact.

Beth sat down at the table with her.

'You're pregnant, aren't you, Beth?' Chloe challenged.

Beth gasped.

'Yes! How did you know?'

'It's written all over your face. Besides, you always drink coffee in the mornings, not chocolate. Congratulations!'

'Well, that was my other bit of news,' Beth explained. 'I haven't told anyone else yet except Lexi.

'I wanted to share it with my closest friends first. I still can't quite believe it!'

'It's very exciting,' Chloe agreed. 'And you know who to call if you need a babysitter!'

'You will be first on my list,' Beth promised.

To Chloe's relief she chatted about the

baby without seeming uncomfortable or awkward.

Chloe couldn't have been happier for her friends. The baby would have a wonderful life here at the villa.

She spent longer talking to Beth than she realised. When Beth dropped her and Gemma back outside the gallery Dominic was looking worried.

'Where were you? I was about to send out a search party!'

He peered at her.

'You look happy.'

'I am,' Chloe assured him.

'Well, this will make you even happier,' Dominic promised. 'We've had a call from someone who wants to buy five of our paintings! How about that?'

'Wonderful!' Chloe replied.

'Even better, one is mine and two are yours!'

'This must be a day for good news.'

Just then her phone rang, bringing her good mood crashing down around her shoulders.

'It's me,' Rob said.

She caught her breath.

'Yes?'

'Good news. We've had an offer on the house. Obviously I wanted to check with you that it's acceptable.'

Chloe froze. Things were moving too fast for her.

'I don't want to know, Rob,' she told him. 'Do whatever you think best.'

'Surely you want some say in it,' he protested.

'I think I lost the right to have any say some time ago,' she responded and ended the call.

Dominic smiled at her gently but said nothing. He just turned and went out the back to put the kettle on.

Chloe suspected that it was going to take more than a cup of tea to revive her good mood.

A Shocking Sight

'Want me to come with you?' Dominic asked as Lexi stood in front of the hall mirror fiddling with her hair. 'For moral support, I mean.'

'No, thanks. I've got to do this on my own. Besides, Beth will be there.'

She couldn't believe how nervous she was about meeting her father. Her party was tomorrow and he'd told Beth, if things went badly, he'd leave Furze Point.

It didn't matter. If things did go badly it would still cast a shadow over Lexi's birthday celebrations.

'I could drive you there,' Dominic offered.

Rachel and Paul came into the hall.

'Or one of us could,' Rachel said. 'You don't have to do this on your own, Lexi.'

'I know, thank you,' Lexi said. 'I'll be fine. I don't know when I'll be back.'

'Take your time,' Rachel said and Lexi saw Paul slip his arm round her.

Their situation wasn't the same but Paul didn't know he had a son until Dominic traced Rachel almost two years ago. It had almost split them up but now they were living as a family.

'We'll be thinking of you,' Rachel said. 'I know and it means a lot to know that. Please don't worry. I can look after myself.'

She hurried out to the van but before she could leave Olly pulled up in his old car.

'Is there a problem?' Lexi asked. 'Has something gone wrong with Midge?'

'Midge is fine. I thought you might like a lift to the villa.'

She looked back and saw Rachel, Paul and Dominic watching from the open doorway.

'I've been offered lifts, thanks. It's kind but I've got to do this myself.'

Olly nodded.

'I thought you'd say that.'

He waved at the others, turned the car round and left.

As she drove towards Laburnum

Villa Lexi turned off into the town. She wanted to take flowers for Beth.

Afterwards, the scent of flowers filling the van, she drove past Chloe and Rob's house.

Chloe was outside with Gemma standing a short distance away.

As Lexi drew to a stop Chloe wrestled with the 'For Sale' sign, swaying the post back and forth until it came out of the ground.

Before Lexi could get to her Chloe smashed the sign on the pavement and jumped on it.

'Chloe! What's going on? Are you OK?'

Chloe's make-up had run down her face and her hair was sticking up. She stared at Lexi as if she didn't know who she was then looked at the mess of wood on the ground.

'What have I done?' she whispered. 'I've ruined everything.'

'It's only a silly old sign,' Lexi soothed. 'Come on, get in the van and I'll run you back to the gallery.'

She shook her head.

'I've got to clear this up!'

'Let me help.'

Together they moved the bits and pieces of wood on to the garden and Chloe began to laugh.

'I don't know what Rob's going to think when he gets home!'

Her laughter turned to tears and Lexi led her to the van.

If only Dominic was at the gallery — she hated leaving Chloe alone.

By the time they got back, however, Chloe had composed herself and insisted she'd be all right.

'I just had to get it out of my system,' she explained. 'I feel much better now. Embarrassed, but better!'

Meeting Martin

'You're late!' Beth said when Lexi drove into the car park outside Laburnum Villa.

Chloe had asked Lexi not to tell anyone what had happened about the sign.

'I was delayed. Here, I got you flowers.'

'They're lovely, thanks. Are you OK?'

Lexi reached down and touched Pongo's head. It was amazing how calming the presence of a dog could be.

'I'm fine. Let's get this over with.'

'It's not meant to be an ordeal!'

'I don't even remember him,' Lexi reminded her. 'I was only two.'

'He used to sit up all night with you when you wouldn't settle. In the armchair with your head on his shoulder. He adores you.'

'Then why did he leave us?'

Beth sighed.

'I explained all that. Come on. He's waiting out the back.'

They went round to the back of the house and Lexi saw him in a grey wicker chair under the awning. He was looking out over the paddocks, watching a child on the back of a grey pony, led by Marie.

He turned and jumped to his feet. Lexi didn't expect him to be so tall, nor so young. Although in his fifties he had a youthful face. He looked . . . nice.

'Lexi!' He came towards her. 'It's wonderful to see you. I've thought about you every day for the past nineteen years.'

He made to hug her but she stepped back so he held out his hand instead. She couldn't move and guilt washed over her as his hand fell to his side.

'Let's all sit down,' Beth suggested.

Martin Clarke reached into his pocket and brought out an old wallet from which he pulled two photos. They were crumpled and scratched but Lexi recognised herself and Beth in one and their mother in the other.

'I never stopped loving you,' he said simply. 'Any of you.'

'You could have come to see us,' Lexi argued.

'I wanted to but your mother thought it best I keep my distance. I used to send money but she returned my cheques.

'I know I did the wrong thing. I've never been happy since.'

His eyes blurred. They were green, like Beth's, Lexi noticed. Kind eyes.

'Did Beth tell you she had to give up university to look after me when Mum was killed?' Lexi challenged angrily.

He lowered his gaze.

'She did, and how she moved here with you and almost lost you.'

He looked tortured.

Although she'd been so young when he left Lexi couldn't help finding him familiar. She had a flash of memory of him singing to her while she was in the bath.

She shook the memory away.

'Why did Mum cut you off from us? I mean, I know what you did because Beth told me, but why make us suffer?'

'She was hurt,' he replied. 'People do

things when they're hurt and it's hard to go back from that.'

She thought of Chloe, smashing up the 'For Sale' sign outside her house.

Chloe had probably gone too far now and it was such a shame. Anyone with half an eye could see those two were meant to be together.

'Beth tells me you live and work at an animal sanctuary,' Martin went on. 'How are you finding it?'

'I love it,' Lexi told him. 'I'm so glad Beth moved us here.'

'You don't wish you'd continued at university? Your sister said you left soon after you started.'

'No, I have no regrets,' Lexi said. 'It wasn't for me.'

'Good. As long as you're happy. That's all that matters.'

'If you hadn't left us we would never have come here,' Lexi mused, remembering what Beth had said earlier. 'Beth wouldn't have met Noah and I may never have ended up working with animals and living at Tiny Tails.'

'That's a good thing, then?' Martin asked tentatively.

'I don't know. We're happy so I guess it is. You just get on with it, don't you?'

They talked some more and she realised that Martin Clarke was a lonely man, one who hadn't been able to move on since leaving his family.

Lexi came to the conclusion that he'd suffered enough.

'Will you be here for my party tomorrow?'

He beamed.

'If you want me to be!'

'I do.' She rose to her feet. 'I'll see you both tomorrow.'

She hesitated for a moment, then held out her hand to shake his.

'It's been nice meeting you. I don't know quite what to call you just yet so, if it's OK, I'll just call you Martin.'

His relieved smile touched her heart.

'That's fine by me.'

'I'll walk you back to your van,' Beth said.

When they'd gone round the side of

the villa Beth hugged her sister.

'Thank you for being so nice to him.'

'It wasn't difficult,' Lexi admitted. 'He's a nice man. I want to get to know him better but that doesn't mean I'll make it easy for him.'

'He's talking about moving here, to Furze Point,' Beth told her. 'Nothing certain just yet. I'm thinking of suggesting he takes over the running of the Beach Hut.

'The guy in there now can only stay until summer, then we have to find someone to replace him.

'How would you feel about that?'

Lexi thought about the beach shop where she and Beth had lived when they first came to Furze Point. Beth had been the caretaker for the beach houses and Lexi had resented it all so much.

She could see their father living there.

'That's a good idea,' she replied. 'I suppose he knows he's going to be a grandad?'

Beth nodded.

'As you know, Noah isn't close to

his parents. I'd love this baby to have a grandparent.'

Lexi could understand that.

Snowfall

The room darkened and Chloe went to the window. The sea was dark grey under a black sky and as she watched, a few flakes of snow drifted down.

It was impossible to see where the sea ended and the sky began. The day of Lexi's twenty-first birthday had an ominous feel to it.

The weather wasn't the only reason for Chloe's sense of foreboding. She had an overwhelming feeling that something bad was going to happen.

As if things could get any worse!

It was only an hour until the party and she'd hoped the cold, but fine, weather would hold for it.

She hurried downstairs to where Rosita and Jamie were packing up the food for the buffet.

'It's snowing,' she informed them.

'What? No, it's not forecast!' Rosita looked out of the window. 'It can't be!'

'It doesn't matter. We'll be under cover

and there are heaters in the marquee,' Jamie soothed. 'Adriana is already there with Lexi and she texted that it's lovely and warm.'

Rosita turned round and looked at Chloe.

'You look great,' she told her. 'Better than great.'

'Thank you,' Chloe replied. 'You two look lovely, too.'

Chloe had used a very good concealer to hide the black bags under her eyes. She was determined to put on a show after what happened yesterday, when she had totally lost it.

Thank goodness only Lexi had witnessed her meltdown outside the house when she'd destroyed the sign.

Today Chloe wasn't feeling very lovely at all. She had only made an effort for Lexi's sake.

The dress she had on was one she'd bought for Rob's cousin's wedding a couple of years before. It was a lovely shade of blue that reminded her of summer evenings.

'How can I help?' she asked.

'You don't have to,' Rosita assured her.

'I know, but I want to.'

'You could take these out to the van,' Jamie suggested. 'Wear a coat!'

A couple of minutes later Chloe came back into the Lighthouse kitchen, her cheeks rosy and her hair sprinkled with snow.

'It's settling,' she announced. 'Will everyone be able to get to the villa?'

'I just heard from Fergus. He has said if it gets bad he plans to clear the way with his tractor. He's not going to let anything ruin Lexi's party.'

'That's our Fergus!' Chloe smiled.

Jamie went out with more food for the van. He came back rubbing his elbow.

'It's pretty slippy out there so mind your step.'

'Did you fall over?' Rosita asked.

'Just once.' He grinned. 'No harm done. We'll load up the excess food into my car so you don't have to make more than one trip, Rosita.'

'Good idea. Chloe, you can come with us.'

'I was going to drive myself,' Chloe replied. 'I don't intend to drink.'

'That doesn't matter,' Rosita argued. 'The fewer cars on the road in this weather the better for everyone.'

She put her arm round Chloe.

'You're part of our family now. We don't leave anyone behind.'

Time to Party

Lexi stood at the front of the marquee, greeting her guests as they arrived. Beth was fluttering around making sure everything was just so.

Martin asked Lexi if she'd mind introducing him to her friends.

'You don't have to say I'm your dad,' he insisted hurriedly.

She laughed.

'I'm not keeping you a secret. I don't care if people know who you are.'

Angela and Olly arrived together, entering in a flurry of snow. Angela shook her umbrella and propped it up just inside the marquee.

'Snow! Can you believe it?' She stepped forward and cupped Lexi's face in her cold hands. 'Happy birthday, darling.'

'I can believe it,' Martin said. 'When Lexi was born the snow was about a foot deep. I thought I was going to have to drag her mother to hospital on a sled!'

Olly laughed.

'You must be Mr Clarke. Pleased to meet you, sir.'

'Call me Martin, please,' he said.

'This is Olly Chapman and his mum, Angela.' Lexi made the introductions.

'You look amazing, Lexi! Such a beautiful young woman, inside and out. I know the invitation said 'no presents' but we couldn't come empty-handed.'

She passed a box to Lexi.

'Shall I open it now?'

'It's up to you,' Olly told her.

'Go on, open it,' Martin advised.

Lexi opened the box. Inside, wrapped beautifully in blue tissue paper, she found a Spode Italian Blue plate, cup and saucer.

'I can't accept this!' Lexi cried. 'It's very good of you but you've already been so generous in donating to Tiny Tails.'

'This is not for Tiny Tails, it's for you,' Angela said. 'It's to start your collection. I want you to use it, though! Have your morning cuppa in it and use the plate for your toast.'

'I don't know if I could,' Lexi protested.

'You should,' Martin said. 'It's too nice to leave sitting on a shelf.'

Lexi hugged Angela and Olly.

'Thank you. It's absolutely gorgeous and I promise I will use it.'

They'd brought Midge along with them, not wanting to leave him alone, and he was keen to say hello to Lexi, too.

The next guests to arrive were Fergus and Anna. They were followed by Nick, Lauren and the children. After that people began to pour in.

Lexi was proud of the way Furze Point welcomed her father, even those who didn't know he'd come back from the dead!

Almost everyone had arrived when Rob turned up with Gemma.

'I hope it was OK to bring her,' he said as he handed Lexi a small parcel. 'I didn't want to leave her at home.

'We have had a bit of vandalism in our road so I thought it best to bring her along.'

Lexi drew in a breath. Was Rob referring to the smashed sign?

He looked around and Lexi was certain he was looking for Chloe but she'd hidden herself away somewhere.

Nevertheless, it was time for the birthday girl to mingle.

'Is it OK to tell them to start the music?' Adriana asked.

'Yes, please,' Lexi replied. 'Let's get this party started!'

Vandalism!

Chloe was uncovering some food when she felt something nudge her leg.

'Gemma? What are you doing here?'

She stroked her then looked round and saw Rob sitting at a nearby table.

He lifted his hand in a wave and she forced herself to smile. She just hoped he didn't have too much to drink this time. She couldn't face another scene.

She walked Gemma back to him.

'Why did you bring her?'

'Funny story. Sit down.'

'Is something wrong?' she asked, complying. 'She's usually OK at home.'

She had to lean in close so he could hear her over the music.

'Strictly speaking it's not really home any more, is it, Chloe?'

She gave him a sharp look but clearly he was just stating a fact.

'I didn't want to leave her there on her own. As I was telling Lexi there's been an incident down our road.'

'What sort of incident?'

'Vandals. I was worried they might come back and Gemma would be scared.'

'Oh, no! What did they do?'

'The house sale sign was damaged, that's all, but you never know what these people might be capable of. Who'd have thought such a thing would happen in Furze Point?'

Chloe felt herself go hot.

'Goodness.' She began to fan her face. 'Is it still snowing?'

He nodded.

'Looks pretty but if it carries on we might all end up stranded here for the night!'

'There are worse places to be stranded.'

It felt strange to be making small talk with Rob as if they barely knew each other.

Still, it was better than things had been lately. At least they weren't pretending any more.

She stood up.

'Help yourself to food.'

'I will.' He looked up at her. 'You look

stunning, by the way.'

'Me? Oh, thank you. You don't look so bad yourself.'

She walked back to the table, sure that he was watching her every move, but when she turned round he was watching others mingle.

How silly to think he'd be interested in her.

'Come and dance, Chloe,' Anna invited and drew her on to the dance floor with Lauren and Beth.

'I really don't want to,' Chloe said but her protests were drowned out by the music.

'Come on! Someone has to start dancing otherwise everyone will sit down all night!' Lauren said.

'What about the children?'

'Casey's with some friends from school and Nick has Caleb,' Lauren said. 'I think it's lovely that there are so many different age groups here.

'Your dad seems nice, Beth.'

'He is!' Beth shouted back.

Try as she might Chloe couldn't stop

looking at Rob. A couple of times Noah and Fergus persuaded him to get up and dance but he went back to his seat at the first opportunity.

Casey's friends left quite early and she latched on to Chloe.

'Has anyone bought my painting yet?' she wanted to know.

'Absolutely not,' Chloe told her. 'It's not for sale. I'm going to keep it for ever! Shall we dance, Casey?'

'Yes, let's dance!'

Chloe couldn't help laughing as the rhythm went through her head. For a while she forgot her troubles and just enjoyed herself.

Casey tugged at her arm and she bent down.

'I need to go to the loo, Auntie Chloe!'

Chloe looked around for Nick or Lauren but they were nowhere to be seen.

'Come on, I'll take you.'

There was a queue at the portable toilets and Casey was already wriggling with her legs crossed.

'Tell you what, we'll nip into the villa,'

Chloe suggested.

'Will that be all right?'

'Yes, of course.'

The snow was quite deep and they giggled as they picked their way across to the house.

Tom was having a patrol round the grounds and waved to them.

'We're just using the facilities!' Chloe called out.

On the way back Casey gathered snow in her hands but it was too soft to make a snowball and she threw it in the air and let it fall over her face.

Lauren took a snapshot in her mind. Casey's upturned face, shining in the outside lights as snow fell back down, would make the most beautiful painting.

'Come on, let's get inside before we freeze!'

'How Dare You?'

They were back at the party in a matter of minutes. As they slipped into the marquee Chloe saw people putting on their coats.

'What's going on?' Chloe asked Lexi's dad. 'Is the party over already?'

'No, it's not that,' Martin said. 'There's a missing child. We're going to look for her.'

'Who is it, do you know?'

He shook his head.

'I'm afraid not.'

Chloe found her coat and looked again for Lauren and Nick so that she could go and help the search.

Holding tight to Casey's hand she joined the throng of people hurrying outside and saw Lauren in floods of tears just ahead.

'What's wrong?' Chloe called out. 'Who is missing?'

'It's Casey!' Lauren sobbed.

'Casey's right here with me!' Chloe

said, dismayed that Lauren was so upset but delighted to be able to reassure her and that Casey wasn't missing.

'Casey!' Lauren almost screamed her name as she pushed her way back through everyone and gathered up her daughter in her arms. 'Where have you been?'

'I just took her to the toilet,' Chloe told her. 'We haven't been gone long.'

Lauren stood up and held Casey tight against her.

'Not long? Have you any idea how long five minutes is when your child is missing? No, of course you don't.

'Why didn't you tell someone you were taking her? And why did no-one in the queue mention that you were there?'

Voices could be heard all around.

'It's OK! She's been found! She's fine.'

Everyone came back into the marquee. The music started up again and it was as if nothing had happened.

'I'm sorry, Lauren. You've hardly seen Casey this evening. I didn't think you'd be worried.'

'What are you saying — that I don't care? I saw her dancing with you earlier and I've been keeping an eye on her.

'How dare you suggest otherwise? Don't come near us!' she said as Nick hurried over.

'What happened?'

'It was Chloe,' Lauren shouted. 'She took Casey!'

'I didn't take her! I'm so sorry. I wouldn't worry you for the world.'

Chloe backed away. It seemed that everyone was staring at her, shaking their heads. She ran for the exit, pushing her way through the people who were returning to the party looking relieved.

Chloe was aghast. She'd upset Lauren but she hadn't meant to, not for one second.

In the car park she remembered she hadn't brought her car. She stopped for a moment, looking round in bewilderment.

Could she walk home? It was a long way at the best of times but would take an age in the snow and she wasn't dressed for it.

Still, going back into the marquee was unthinkable. She trudged on down the long road that took her past the back of the beach houses and the Beach Hut shop.

Her feet were sore and ached with the cold and her hands tingled. She had no hat, no gloves and just a dress on under her padded jacket. She felt cold to her bones.

Her thoughts were jumbled. She'd have to leave Furze Point and make a clean break. Go somewhere that no-one knew her.

Right now she was the awful woman who had left that lovely Rob Marsden and then had taken a child!

Her feet went from under her and she landed face down in the snow, sobbing, feeling as if her heart would break.

As the cold enveloped her she thought she might never get up. It would be so easy just to lie here and let the snow cover her.

It was already starting again, fat flakes

drifting down.

She felt hands holding her, gently pulling her to her feet. Then she felt the familiar nuzzle of a gentle nose.

'Gemma,' she whispered tearfully. 'Rob? What are you doing here?'

'Looking for you,' he told her. 'You can't walk home in this.

'Come back to the villa and I'll drive you home.'

'Home?' she echoed.

Would Rosita want her at the Lighthouse after what she had done tonight? Would she still say that she was part of their family?

She cuffed at her tears.

'Either the Lighthouse or wherever you want to go, Chloe,' Rob replied. 'Noah told me what happened.'

She shook her head.

'Why would you want anything to do with me?'

'Because you're still my wife — and I love you,' he said simply.

'Even though I kidnapped a child tonight?'

236

He laughed incredulously.

'Of course you didn't kidnap anyone,' he said. 'You took Casey to the toilet, that's all.

'Tom told us that he saw Casey prancing round with her legs crossed and you running up to the villa with her when he was having a check round.

'He didn't get back to the party to tell us all that until after you'd run off, unfortunately.'

'I scared Lauren, though,' Chloe whispered.

'Lauren is fine,' Rob assured her. 'She's mortified that she snapped at you, that's all. It was fear talking.

'Everyone knows you didn't mean to frighten her. Come back to the party or, if you insist on leaving, then I'll drive you. I'm not letting you walk in this.'

Chloe didn't want to go back to the party but said she'd accept a lift. They were halfway back up the road when she saw Lauren running towards them.

'Chloe, thank goodness! I've been worried about you!

'I'm so sorry for speaking to you like that. Casey said, if it wasn't for you, she would have had an accident. I can't imagine how much that would have upset her. She'd have been mortified.'

'I'm sorry, too, Lauren.' Chloe began to cry again. 'She was in such a hurry I didn't want to make her wait.'

'I know, and you saw Tom and probably assumed he'd tell us where Casey was.'

'I suppose I did.'

'Please come back to the party!' Lauren begged. 'Everyone is worried about you. We all love you.'

'Yes, do,' Rob urged. 'Just come back in long enough to warm up. Perhaps we could have a dance.'

Chloe laughed and choked.

'You and me?'

'There's no-one else I'd want to dance with, Chloe. Ever.'

He put his arm round her and she leaned against him.

This was so silly, she thought. She had to keep up her tough act but it was difficult when she had mascara all over her face and her tears and the snow had washed the concealer away from her eyes.

'I must look a fright,' she fretted.

'You look beautiful.'

When they returned to the party it was as if nothing had happened. People were dancing, laughing, eating and drinking.

Lexi came over with two plates bearing generous portions of birthday cake.

'I thought you were going to miss out,' she said. 'Can't have that!'

'Please Come Home'

At Rob's table he took his jacket off and draped it round Chloe's shoulders. It felt warm and smelled comfortingly of him.

'Your coat should be dry by the time you go home. If not you can wear mine.'

She nodded and he pressed a drink in her hand.

'No, thanks,' she said.

'It's just a small brandy,' he urged. 'Pretend I'm a Saint Bernard.'

'That's a myth, Rob. They don't carry barrels of brandy round their necks.'

'Well, there might be some truth in it,' he argued. 'I read that a worker in a Swiss museum hung his wine barrel round the neck of a stuffed dog . . .'

'Stuffed dog?' Chloe pulled a face.

'Hero dog,' he amended. 'Anyway, something like that.'

She laughed. This was how things used to be. She'd pull Rob's leg about all the things he seemed to know. He soaked up facts like a sponge and loved sharing his knowledge.

He really ought to have children to share it with . . .

Her face fell. What was she doing, letting her guard down like this?

'Stop,' Rob said. 'Take that look off your face. My Chloe was back for a minute; please don't leave again.'

'I'm not back, Rob.' She took a sip of the brandy. 'I can never come back.'

'Was I something I did?'

'No. I can't tell you.'

'Don't you think I have a right to know?'

Of course he did. She swallowed the rest of the brandy.

'I want you to start a new life and marry someone who can give you children.'

His mouth dropped open.

'That's it?'

'Yes!' She felt offended that he was being so casual.

'You think I married you for the children you might have?' he demanded.

She shrugged. When they'd married, children had been the last thing on their minds. They'd never even discussed having a family.

It was only later that it became an obsession. The more disappointments they had the more determined they became to succeed.

'I know you didn't.'

It felt surprisingly good to have this out in the open, to explain herself to him. She hoped it would help him understand and eventually accept what had to be.

'You're great with kids, Rob,' she went on. 'You'd make a wonderful dad.'

Rob looked around him, then rubbed his hand across his eyes.

'Do you think Fergus would make a wonderful dad?'

'Definitely.' She nodded.

'So do you think he and Anna should split up if that doesn't happen?'

'Well, no.'

'How about Beth and Noah?'

'It's a little late for that question,' she confided. 'Don't tell anyone, though!'

'That's fantastic news! I'm so pleased for them.

'But can't you see what I'm saying? I married you because I loved you. I still love you. I love our home and our way of life and this daft dog.

'I even loved you when you had me on that diet and I had to sneak off regularly to the Beach Hut for bacon sandwiches!'

She laughed but then stopped. This was no laughing matter, it was serious.

She remembered something else.

'What about the house, Rob? You put it up for sale. You must have felt ready to move on.'

He shook his head.

'I've never felt less ready for anything in my life. I put it up for sale hoping it would shock you into coming home.

'I thought, if you had to go round it choosing from things we've bought together over the years, it might bring you to your senses.

'I'm sorry, it was a stupid thing to do and it backfired anyway because you said you didn't want anything.'

'Only because it would hurt too much,' she confessed. 'What about the offer?'

'What offer?' He laughed. 'The agent said I hadn't a hope of getting any interest at the price I put it up for sale.'

'Oh, Rob, what a silly thing to do.'

'Well, desperation drives you to silly things,' he said. 'Like the person that smashed the 'For Sale' board.

'It was all caught on our neighbour's CCTV, by the way.'

Chloe swallowed.

'Was it?'

He reached across the table and grasped her cold hand in his.

'Mrs Murdoch called me over to show me.'

'I expect it was all fuzzy and blurry and you couldn't see the culprit,' Chloe said hopefully.

'Oh, I saw her fine,' he said. 'She looked absolutely demented!

'I also saw Lexi's van pull up and her helping you clear the mess away.'

'I'm sorry.' She hung her head.

'No, Chloe, I'm sorry. It was a stupid thing to do — I see that now. All we needed was to talk to each other, like we are now.'

'You wouldn't talk to me!'

'And you wouldn't talk to me,' he countered. 'What a pair we are.'

'You once said we could adopt,' she said. 'That's when I realised that having a child meant as much to you as it did to me, possibly more.'

'Chloe, if you wanted to adopt I'd want to as well. If you're happy to stay as we are then so am I. All I care about is that we're together.

'It's what couples do — face challenges together. No-one knows what life is going to throw at them. I could be injured on a shout. You could fall flat on your face in the snow and end up looking like a panda. Who knows?'

Gemma rested her heavy head in Chloe's lap.

'You know what she's saying, don't you?' he said. 'She wants you to come home. So do I.'

Chloe was vaguely aware that the music had stopped as she squeezed Rob's hand.

Perfect

The party was almost over, with few people left. Chloe was in Rob's arms, swaying to the music as he held her tight as if he'd never let her go.

A hand touched her back and she turned.

'We're going home now,' Rosita said. 'Shall I give you a key or . . . ?'

'No need. I'll pick my car up tomorrow.'

'Thank goodness for that!' Rosita whooped. 'Congratulations. Not that I haven't loved having you to stay but you know where you belong.'

When the music stopped Chloe looked around. Lexi was laughing and enjoying her special day with Olly, Dominic and her father. She had had doubts about meeting him but it seemed to be going well.

Chloe's sense of despair had vanished. For the first time in ages she had a different sort of hope in her heart.

246

It wasn't for the future she'd longed for but a different kind of future. One that could be just as happy.

'Time to go.' Rob retrieved her coat.

They said their goodbyes and left with Gemma trotting happily at their heels.

The sky had cleared and the snow sparkled in the moonlight.

'Isn't this the most perfect night?' Chloe marvelled.

Rob bent to kiss her.

'It is now.'

We do hope that you have enjoyed reading this large print book.

Did you know that all of our titles are available for purchase?

We publish a wide range of high quality large print books including:
Romances, Mysteries, Classics
General Fiction
Non Fiction and Westerns

Special interest titles available in large print are:
The Little Oxford Dictionary
Music Book, Song Book
Hymn Book, Service Book

Also available from us courtesy of Oxford University Press:
Young Readers' Dictionary
(large print edition)
Young Readers' Thesaurus
(large print edition)

For further information or a free brochure, please contact us at:
Ulverscroft Large Print Books Ltd.,
The Green, Bradgate Road, Anstey,
Leicester, LE7 7FU, England.
Tel: (00 44) **0116 236 4325**
Fax: (00 44) **0116 234 0205**

Other titles in the
Linford Romance Library:

CHRISTMAS AT MALDINGTON

Anne Stenhouse

When famous presenter Genni Kilpatrick watches someone die in front of her on live TV, she has a mental breakdown. In a bid to escape public scrutiny, she flees to Maldington House in search of inner peace. But between her following entourage and the local pantomime production, serenity remains elusive. Will she finally find it in the arms of local electrician Paddy Delford?

MURDER AT THE ABBEY

Sue Cook

1536. Abbey cook Agnes Morrow nurses a secret that she dares not let Abbot Mark de Winter discover . . . not yet, anyway. Not until she is sure he is ready for it. But then King Henry VIII's men come to strip the abbey of its treasures, and two murders threaten to destroy all her hopes. Will her future happiness be torn asunder, or will her long-cherished dreams come true?

THE HIDDEN TRUTH

John Darley

The Second World War might be over, but Cheryl is still battling with its consequences. Each day she has to keep a secret, shared only with her sister. Then, when she finds herself unwittingly falling in love with a young doctor she works with at the hospital, she feels she can no longer bear to continue living a lie. But what choice does she have? Can she ever tell the truth? She longs for peace . . . but at what price?